3.07 p.m. on a sunny Saturday . . .

CHAPTER ONE

KIND OF A BIG DEAL

'Finn? Can I talk to you for a second?'

My best friend in the whole world, Isha Kapesa, is standing over me, her fingers tapping the comic strip I'm drawing.

I blink and look up. Ten seconds ago I was lost in my own cartoon fantasy world. And now I'm right back in my bedroom at 3.07 p.m. on a sunny Saturday.

'Isha!' I drop my pen as I stand up to give her a hug. 'Check it out – I'm just finishing up our latest comic!'

Because, you see, Isha Kapesa is not JUST my best friend in the whole world – she's also my writing partner. Together, we are FINNTASMO-ISHAZAR COMICS: makers of the awesomest, pawesomest, most LAUGH-OUT-LOUDEST cartoon adventures around!

You've probably heard of us. We're kind of a big deal.

Everyone at school loves our madcap comics about our three wild 'n' wacky characters – ARLEY, TAPPER and JENNY WEATHERLEGS!

'So what's up, Isha?' I ask.

She shifts on the spot and frowns. Which is super weird, because Isha is usually rocking the BIGGEST smile you've ever seen. 'I just got this note through my door,' she says, holding up a tattered piece of paper. Her voice drops to a whisper: 'It's from Zack Jellicoe . . .'

'WHAT?!'

← Zack Jellicoe

This is brain-frazzlingly BANANAS for many reasons – the main one being that Zack Jellicoe is a CARTOON CHARACTER.

To be precise, he's my FAVOURITE cartoon character.

Four Zack facts for you:

1 Zack is a crime-fightin', skateboardin', shades-wearin' SUPER-DUDE.

↑ Yorky

2 Zack was created by a cartoonist called Yorky, who used to be my total hero until I found out he was a beardy wrong'un who nicks other people's ideas (it's a long story).

3 Zack has been trapped here in the Real World ever since Yorky tried to erase him (another long story).

4 Zack thinks Isha and me can help him get back home to Toon World . . .

See, he tracked us down last week, because he'd heard

about how Arley and Tapper had magically appeared in the Real World too, before me and Isha managed to send them back (that one's the longest story yet).

He said he'd be in touch soon because he had a plan. And now he's sent us this note . . .

'So what does it say?' I ask.

Isha hands it to me:

Dear Finn & Isha,

I may have finally found a way home to Toon World. But I need your help. Meet me tomorrow at midday at King Ubu's Comic Book Store, 16 Sweeney Terrace, London, and I'll explain everything.

The Lost Toons are counting on you . . .

Yours desperately,

Zack Jellicoe

I look up, my eyes boggling in amazement. '"The Lost Toons"?' I hiss. 'I thought it was just him?'

Isha shrugs. 'I guess we'll find out.'

'We've got to help him, right?'

She nods. 'Of course. And London's not far – my sister can drive us there tomorrow.'

Isha's big sister Mona is seventeen and has just passed her driving test. She's great, Mona. Very pretty. I mean, not that I've noticed, or anything. She just is. But, anyway. Let's change the subject.

Is it hot in here?

I jump up from my chair. I'm so pumped with the excitement of what tomorrow might bring that I've NO CLUE how I'll survive the next twenty-four hours. But then I remember something that ALWAYS takes my mind off stuff: drawing cartoons!

'Shall we keep going on our latest comic?' I ask Isha, grabbing my sketchbook. 'Check out the lightning bolts I drew shooting out of Jenny Weatherlegs' toes! I just need to finish the final frame. How do you think it should end?'

I'm grinning at her with my widest, brightest grin. Honestly, there is NOTHING I love more than making

Arley, Tapper & Jenny cartoons with Isha!

But she's not grinning back. She's still shifting on the spot and frowning.

What is going on here?

'Actually, Finn,' she says, 'before we start, there's something else I need to tell you too . . .'

'OK. What is it?'

She stares at the floor. 'I didn't want to say anything until it was official, but Mum and Dad finally told me last night that it's happening.'

'*What's* happening?'

She looks me in the eye. 'I'm moving.'

CHAPTER TWO

LOS ANGELES, NORWICH

'Oh . . . OK.' I shrug. 'Well, that's all right. So we won't live on the exact same street any more. Where are you moving to? Mathers Terrace? De Selby Grove?'

Isha's eyes are back on the carpet. 'A bit further than that,' she murmurs. 'My dad's been offered a new job . . . in Los Angeles.'

I almost laugh. She's joking. She *must* be. 'Los

Angeles . . . in AMERICA?'

She half smiles. 'No, Finn, Los Angeles in *Norwich*.'
And then the half-smile fades and I know for sure she's
not joking.

'But . . . But . . .'

It's weird: I'm standing completely still, but it feels
like I'm falling. Off a SUPER high cliff. My tummy is
drooping and swooping and my eyes start to sting as
a horrible thought burns itself on to my brain: *I might
never see Isha again.*

And then I'm not falling any more – it's like I've hit
the ground and splattered into a million, trillion pieces.

Isha is the best friend I've ever had. She's the kind of
friend I didn't know it was even *possible* to have. The
kind where you don't even have to speak – it's like you
can read each other's minds. The kind you never have
to pretend with, because their favourite version of you
is the Real You.

She has the greatest comic book knowledge of any
person on this planet. She's funny and brave and clever
and comes up with the most AWESOMELY BANANAS

ideas for cartoons. Ideas I could NEVER think of. When I'm making comics with Isha, I'm the happiest I've ever been – both of us laughing like drains as we create wild stories about our beloved characters together.

She's staring at me now. It's my turn to speak. But my throat feels like it's full of extra-gloopy honey, and I'm worried how my voice will sound. So all I say is:

'Oh. Right.'

She wrinkles her nose sadly, like she wanted me to say something more. 'We can still carry on making comics together, though,' she says quietly. 'If you want.'

If you want. She's only saying that because she feels sorry for me. She'll be swanning around Los Angeles with her cool new American friends. Why would she want to keep drawing cartoons with uncool old ME, thousands of miles away?

I shrug. I don't want her to see how sad I am. 'Whatever.'

She takes a deep breath and nods. I want to grab her and hug her and BEG her not to go. But I'm worried that would make me look like a total WEIRDO. So I just keep quiet.

And, for the first time in our friendship, it's not that easy, comfy, reading-each-other's-mind silence. This one feels jagged and cold and wrong.

Like something's broken and it might never get fixed.

CHAPTER THREE

KING UBU'S COMIC BOOK STORE

Things feel even *wrong*-er the next day.

It's absolutely CHUCKING it down with rain, and for the whole car journey into London, Mona goes on about how 'cool' it will be living in California, and all the 'awesome' stuff she and Isha will do. Isha sits next to me, staring out the window and saying nothing. And I start to feel not just sad any more, but . . . angry.

Because Isha obviously doesn't CARE about being friends with me. I bet she was jumping for joy when her mum and dad told her they were moving away.

Well, whatever, I tell myself sternly. *Who needs her?*

'Here we are, then!' Mona calls, as she parks the car. 'Sixteen Sweeney Terrace!'

We get out and she tells us she'll wait in the car for us. The rain has stopped now, and the sun's poking its head out from behind the clouds. I spot the shop where we're supposed to meet Zack straight away – its sign is all cracked and faded:

KING UBU'S COMIC BOOK STORE

'I've never even *heard* of this comic shop,' Isha says.

'Me neither.'

'Weird . . .'

We walk across to the store. The sun is out properly

now, and a mega-sized glistening rainbow is stretching across the sky above us. Isha looks up at it and smiles. 'Hey – that reminds me of a cool idea I had for *one of our comics*! I was thinking Jenny Weatherlegs could—'

She catches my eye and stops talking. Her smile disappears and I feel a cold stinging pain like an ICICLE through my chest. One of our comics. We probably won't ever make another comic together again.

I wait to see if Isha will finish her sentence.

'Doesn't matter,' she mutters.

I bite the inside of my cheek. That same thought runs through my head again: *Whatever. Who needs her?*

I push the door of King Ubu's. But it's locked.

Isha knocks. There's a shuffling noise from inside, then a muffled, high-pitched voice hisses: **'What's the password?'**

We look at each other. 'Er . . . we weren't given a password,' Isha says.

'OK,' the voice shoots back. **'I'll give you a clue. The password rhymes with "minky mums".'**

Isha wrinkles her forehead. 'Inky . . . sums?'

'Nope,' says the voice.

'Dinky plums?' I try.

'Not even close.'

Isha scratches her head. 'What about . . . *stinky bums?*'

There's a second of silence. Then we hear a ROAR of hysterical laughter. **'Wah-ha-ha-ha!!'** the voice cackles. **'There IS no password! I just wanted to see if I could make you say "stinky bums"! And I DID! Wah-ha-ha!!!'**

Isha rolls her eyes. 'Look, we haven't got time for this—'

'YOU SAID "STINKY BUMS"!!! WAH-HA-HA!'

'CAN YOU SHUT IT, PLEASE!' Isha shouts. 'We're here to see Zack Jellicoe!'

'All right, all right,' snaps the voice. **'Honestly, where's your sense of humour?'**

We hear the CLICK-CLACK-CLUNK of a heavy lock, and then the door opens to reveal . . . a cartoon tiger in a karate kit.

CHAPTER FOUR

THE LOST TOONS

'**H**iya!' says the cartoon tiger. '**I'm Tyger Stylez. With a "y" in "Tyger" and a "z" in "Stylez". As you can see, I'm a tiger but I'm also schooled in twenty-six different martial arts. Imagine that!**' He chuckles and then pounces into a pretty impressive kung-fu kick. '**You must be the famous Finntasmo and Ishazar? The ones that sent Arley and Tapper back to Toon World!**'

Me and Isha just nod, our mouths hanging wide wide WIDE open. I thought Zack was the only Toon still hiding out in the Real World! What the **MONKEY NUTS** is going on here?!

'Come in and meet the gang!' Tyger Stylez yanks us through the door and into the shop.

King Ubu's obviously used to be a proper comic store – but that must have been a long LONG time ago. There are racks and shelves and a till and faded posters of the X-Men and Black Panther. But the walls are covered in browny-green moss, the place smells like mouldy eggs and it's totally empty. Until—

'Finn! Isha!'

Zack Jellicoe comes zipping towards us on his skateboard! **'I knew you'd come!'** He beams. **'I see you've already met Tyger Stylez . . .'**

'I did the old password trick on them,' Tyger Stylez chuckles. **'Got them to say "Stinky bums"! CLASSIC banter!'**

'Yes, very amusing, Tyger,' Zack sighs.

'Zack, what is going on?' Isha asks, her eyes still

WIBBLING in disbelief. 'We thought it was only YOU that was stuck here?'

Zack shakes his head. **'I'm afraid not. There are others – like Tyger here. We were all leading happy and fulfilled lives in Toon World. And then our Artists stopped drawing us, and we were zapped here – lost, frightened and alone. Well . . . not quite alone. We all live here together in secret – in this abandoned comic shop.'**

He puts his arm around Tyger and smiles at us. His ONLY arm. I probably should've mentioned that: Zack's only got one arm. His evil Artist, Yorky, rubbed the other one out. (I'll say it again: BEARDY WRONG'UN.)

'This is too, too wild,' I murmur, looking at the two living, breathing Toons in front of me.

'But where are my manners!' Zack exclaims. **'You need to meet the rest of the gang.'** He whistles loudly, and from the back of the shop emerges the most mind-scramblingly WEIRD-O-RIFIC bunch of cartoon characters I've ever seen: a fire-breathing little old lady, a dude in a onesie holding a giant ladder, and a RASPBERRY wearing a bow tie!

'Finn and Isha - these are the Lost Toons!' Zack says. 'All of us got trapped here in the Real World after our Artists stopped drawing us. I met Tyger first, then we ran into GranZilla and Ladder Man.'

'Hello, dearies!' roars GranZilla, setting fire to her knitting.

'My superpower is that I have a really big ladder,' says Ladder Man cheerfully.

'And finally we found Berry Vinefeld,' Zack says. 'Berry is a stand-up comedian whose jokes are exclusively about summer fruits.'

GranZilla →

← Berry Vinefeld

Berry Vinefeld waddles towards us, grinning. **'Hey, good evening, ladies and gentlemen, what a great audience. Here – what do you call a strawberry and a raspberry playing guitar together? I'll tell you – A JAM SESSION! Thank you, thank you, I'm here all week.'**

Zack leans in and whispers: **'I can see why Berry's Artist gave up on him, to be honest. He's fairly annoying.'**

Suddenly – KA-BLOOM!!! – there's a mahoosive EXPLOSION from the door behind the till. Me and Isha nearly jump out of our socks: 'What was that?!'

Zack laughs. **'Right on cue. Here's who I REALLY brought you here to meet.'**

The door opens and out steps easily the most WEIRD-O-RIFIC member of the whole gang . . . I don't even know how to describe her. It's like a horse, a fish and a science teacher have been put in a blender. And then the blender has EXPLODED.

'This,' says Zack, **'is Kate Magenta Great Inventor!'**

'Apologies,' says Kate Magenta Great Inventor, dusting herself off. **'Experiment went slightly haywire. I must've**

mixed up the nitric acid and lemon juice.' She trots towards us with a goofy smile. **'Anyway - greetings, Real Worlders! Glad to make your acquaintance!'**

Zack clocks the utterly butterly BAMBOOZLED looks on mine and Isha's faces and chuckles. **'Kate is part-llama, part-dolphin, part-eagle, part-brilliant scientist.'**

'It seems my Artist was fairly indecisive,' she sighs. **'So, tell me - did you two really manage to send two Toons back home?'**

I nod, and there is a flutter of excitement among the Lost Toons.

'You hear that, lads?' Tyger shouts. **'We're going home!'**

'We all miss Toon World desperately, you see, dearies,' GranZilla tells us.

Ladder Man nods: **'It's no life for a Toon here in the Real World.'**

'But listen,' I say. 'We only managed to get Arley and Tapper back because I am their Artist. Only an Artist can send their own Toons back to Toon World, and I'm not your Artist!'

   'Don't worry about that,' Kate Magenta chuckles.
'I've worked out a way to get around that particular
little glitch.'

   'How?'

   Kate grins. 'I'm glad you asked. With THIS . . .'

   And she holds up what might be a pen – or a firework.

CHAPTER FIVE

THE MAGIC PEN

'**I**t's Kate's latest invention,' Zack says proudly. '**The Magic Pen!**'

Kate hands it to me. '**I've spent months designing it. All we need is a genuine Real World comic book team to draw us with it, and we'll all be zapped back home. In a jiffy!**'

Me and Isha stare at the RIDONKULOUS pen with our mouths open. 'What's it made of?' Isha asks.

'Mostly ink and plastic,' Kate says. 'Some wires. Bit of Blu Tack. A squeeze of lemon juice. Big old splash of nitric acid. Half a Twix. Two tablespoons of dynamite. A fair bit of plutonium. Probably went a bit overboard on the plutonium, if I'm honest.'

'Riiiiiight,' I say. 'And it definitely works?'

'Oh, yeah.' Kate nods. 'Definitely. I'm, like, ninety per cent sure it works.'

'Ninety per cent isn't definite,' Isha points out.

'OK, call it eighty-five,' Kate says cheerily. 'Eighty, tops.'

'I'm not sure about this, Finn,' Isha whispers. And to be totally honest, I'm not sure either. But right now, something's making me want to do the exact OPPOSITE of whatever Isha says. I'm going to have to get used to doing stuff without her once she's swanned off to Los Angeles, aren't I? So why not start now?

Feeling a jolt of anger, I grab a piece of paper. 'OK, I'll start drawing.'

'Super!' cries Kate.

'Wahoooo!' bellows Tyger Stylez.

'Finn,' Isha hisses. 'I think we should talk about this. That pen doesn't look safe . . .'

'Whatever.' I start sketching Zack Jellicoe's outline with it.

'We should make this decision together,' Isha says sharply. 'We're supposed to be a team, remember?'

Another icy blast of anger thumps into my chest. 'Yeah, well, you've made it pretty clear you don't WANT us to be a team any more, haven't you?'

She looks at me, her eyes wide and shiny. 'What's that supposed to mean?'

I ignore her and keep sketching.

'Finn, seriously . . .'

The pen starts to splutter and fizz, sparks flying out of it like mini-fireworks . . .

'Don't worry, that's supposed to happen!' Kate shouts. **'Probably!'**

'Finn, stop!' Isha begs.

But I don't. I keep drawing. And the pen keeps sparking, quicker and louder and sparkier by the second. Even Kate is looking worried now. But all I can think about is Isha leaving, and how we won't draw Arley and Tapper and Jenny any more, and suddenly I don't care about anything else.

'FINN!!!'

I feel Isha grab the pen off me. But it's too late. The sparks are EVERYWHERE, exploding around us so fast I can barely see. The whole world suddenly feels like it's made of rubber, bending and wobbling around me. And then . . .

ZZZZZAPPPPPPP!!!!!!

There's nothing but darkness.

CHAPTER SIX

WHERE ARE WE?!

'**F**inn? Finn?'

Isha's voice.

'What happened?' she whispers. 'Where are we?!'

I open my eyes. But I can't see anything. It's completely pitch BLACK.

I can FEEL something, though. I'm moving.

Very gently and veeeeeeery slowly, like I'm on a giant

version of that conveyor belt thing Mum and Dad put their shopping on in the supermarket.

'What is going on?!' Isha hisses, next to me. 'What is this?'

'I don't know . . .'

Behind us, I can hear other voices now. I can't make out what they're saying, but there are a lot of them. A REAL lot.

'I don't like this, Finn . . .' I hear Isha say.

'Me neith—'

Suddenly a super-loud, robotic voice rings out above us:

YOU ARE NOW APPROACHING THE ARRIVALS GATE! PLEASE MIND THE GAP! YOU ARE NOW APPROACHING THE ARRIVALS GATE!

The voices behind us get even louder and more excited. My tummy does about six SQUILLION backflips. 'Arrivals gate?' *Where the* MONKEY NUTS *are we arriving?*

The robotic voice rings out again:

ARRIVING IN
THREE . . . TWO . . .
ONE . . .

And then . . . LIGHT.

So much light that I STILL can't see what's happening.

I rub my stinging eyes as what feels like a hundred people start pushing past me, all of them shouting, **'Excuse me!'** and **'Mind out!'** and **'Coming through!'**

I blink hard, and the world FINALLY swims into focus.

But it's not the same world. It's different.

It takes my FRAZZLED brain a few seconds to figure out what's wrong. Everything here is sketchy and scribbly. Everything is super-bright and colourful. Everything is two-dimensional.

Everything is . . . CARTOON.

This time, my stomach does SIXTY squillion backflips.

All the people pushing past us – they're not people.
They're TOONS.

They're all different shapes and sizes – some are tiny doodled stick men, some are GIGANTORIFIC full-colour animals, others are monsters, lamp posts, dinosaurs, chocolate bars and pretty much every other thing you can think of!

My tummy buckles like I'm on a busted roller coaster. I look round at Isha. Her mouth is hanging WIDE open as she stares ahead of us.

'Where the absolute **MONKEY NUTS** are we?' I whisper. I'm not expecting an answer, but I get one. We look up to see a CARTOON RABBIT in a smart uniform sat at a desk above us.

'Welcome to Toon World,' he says. **'What is the purpose of your visit?'**

WELCOME TO TOON WORLD

CHAPTER SEVEN

YOU ARE NOW ENTERING TOON WORLD

'**T**OON WORLD?!' Isha's eyes look like they might pop out of her head.

'This . . . this can't be happening?' I stammer. 'Can it?'

'It both can and is, young feller-me-lad,' says the rabbit, leaning over his desk to look at us. 'Right here is where all new Toons arrive after they've been drawn for the first time.'

'But we're . . . WE'RE NOT TOONS!' Isha yells, as a roaring T-Rex stomps past, nearly squishing all three of us.

The rabbit squints at Isha and me. **'Hmm. Yes. Now you mention it, you do look a bit threedy-measurable.'**

'Three-dimensional . . .' I murmur, as the T-Rex takes a big CHOMP out of the 'WELCOME TO TOON WORLD' sign.

'That's the one,' says the rabbit. **'Well, don't worry – if you're not supposed to be here, you'll get rubbed out in a second. Happens to about half the new arrivals that come through. Have a look . . .'**

Our eyes follow where his paw is pointing. It's true – half the Toons rushing through the Arrivals Gate are CHANGING right in front of us! Either they're being RUBBED OUT, or they're having new ARMS and LEGS and HEADS added to them! It's like they're being drawn and re-drawn before our very eyes! I gawp at them, too flabber-gobsmacked even to speak.

'Who's DOING that to them?' Isha gasps.

'Their Artists, obviously,' the rabbit says. **'Everything**

you see in Toon World is drawn by an Artist somewhere – even me!'

I gawp at Isha and she gawps right back. This is too, TOO bananas.

'Anyway, you two,' the rabbit says. 'I haven't got all day. What is the purpose of your visit here?' He leans over and whispers. 'Don't worry, I'm not picking on you – we have to ask everybody that now. Orders of the new Toon president, Mr Bill Dozer!'

On the next desk, a talking TOMATO in the same uniform as the rabbit chips in: 'Ooh, I do like that nice president Dozer! He seems like a lovely man!'

'Yes, Margerie, we all love President Dozer,' agrees the rabbit. 'So – what are you two doing here?'

Me and Isha look at each other. 'Well . . . we were drawing something with this magical pen—' I start.

But Isha cuts me

off. '*You* were drawing something. *I* told you to stop.'

I feel a flicker of anger in my tummy as I remember that she's DITCHING me for Los Angeles.

'We don't know what we're doing here,' she tells the rabbit. 'But we need to get home. Back to the Real World.'

The rabbit takes his cap off and scratches his ears. 'Hmm. Well, if you want to go anywhere, you should try Toon Central Station. It's just through that door, by the map . . .'

CHAPTER EIGHT

TOON CENTRAL STATION

'Doodle Broadway, Scribble Junction, Sketching Gardens . . .' I shake my head. 'This is all just too, TOO wild.'

We are staring at the mahoosive map of Toon World inside the train station. On either side of us, trains – huge cartoon trains with cartoon FACES – keep hissing into the platforms, letting all manner of weird, wacky and wonderful Toons on and off. Most of them giggle and point at Isha and me as they walk past. Some even stop and take pictures. I guess to them, WE'RE the oddball weirdos.

'**'Scuse me,**' says a passing great white shark. '**Could my wife and I have a selfie with you? You're just so darn-tootin' STRANGE-lookin'!**'

'**Yes,**' says his great white shark wife. '**Kind of Threedy-Measurable.**'

We stand there as they take the picture. Then Isha turns back to the map.

'How are we supposed to know which way to go?' she asks, as the latest train toots its whistle and rumbles away.

I shake my head. 'No idea.'

She shoots me an irritated glance. 'So, we're stuck here, then.'

'Why are you looking at me like that?' I shoot back. 'It's not my fault, is it?'

She throws her hands up in the air. 'Not your fault?! Finn, I *told* you that pen was bad news. But did you listen?'

I feel the hairs on the back of my neck start to tingle. Why is SHE getting annoyed with ME?! I only used that stupid pen because I was so angry at her for moving away!

'Whatever,' I snap.

This just seems to make her MORE annoyed.

'"Whatever"?' she echoes. '"Whatever"?! I just nearly got squished by a T-Rex, and we're now stuck in this weird-o-rific cartoon dimension with no way back, and all you can say is "Whatever"! My sister's sitting outside King Ubu's, waiting for us right now! She's gonna be worried SICK! And it's all your fault, Finn!'

'What's the matter, Isha?' I sneer. 'Are you worried you're going to miss your flight to "Los Angeles"?' I do a silly voice and finger quote marks around 'Los Angeles', as if it's a stupid, ridiculous, babyish place.

'WHAT?!' Isha scruffles her hair in frustration, as another train hisses into the platform behind her. 'What has me moving to America got to do with any of this?'

'It's got EVERYTHING to do with it!' My eyes feel

hot again now, and my voice is getting wibbly.

'Well, you didn't seem very bothered about me leaving when I told you yesterday!' she shouts. 'I don't get why you suddenly care so much now!'

'I DON'T care! You can leave tomorrow as far as I'm concerned!' I don't even know what I'm saying. The words are just tumbling out of my mouth. What I WANT to say is: '*OF COURSE I care! It's all I've been thinking about for the last twenty-four hours! You're my best friend in the whole world and I don't want to lose you!*' But some STOOPID, try-hard, wannabe-tough part of my brain has taken control and is doing the talking for me.

'Finn, you're being a total numpty,' Isha hisses.

'No, YOU'RE the numpty!' I fire back.

A cartoon postbox sticks its square red head in between us. **'Excuse me – I was wondering if I could get a selfie with you–'**

'NO!' we both shout.

'Sheesh, sorry.' The postbox slinks away.

Isha's eyes are back on me, BLAZING with fury. 'If

that's how you feel, Finn, then maybe it's a good thing I'm moving away. Maybe it's for the best that Finntasmo-Ishazar Comics is coming to an end.'

'Fine by me!' the STOOPID part of my brain yells. 'I was happier making comics on my own anyway!'

This is a lie. A ridonkulous lie. The most doughnut-headedly ridonkulous lie I've ever told. I want to take it straight back. But I don't. Isha's bottom lip wobbles, and she bites it hard.

'Oh, *really*?' she says. It's like she's teasing me. DARING me to go further.

'Yes, really!' I shout. 'I don't need you! I never have!'

The Toons on the platform are all staring at us now – and not just because we're the only threedy-measurable things in sight. But I don't care. All I can think about is how ANGRY I am that Isha's abandoning me. That she obviously doesn't care about me or Arley or Tapper or Jenny Weatherlegs, and she's happy to DITCH all of us to go and live on the other side of the world.

'OH, IS THAT HOW IT IS?!' Isha yells, even louder. I might be imagining it, but I'm sure I see a tiny sparkly tear form in each of her brown eyes. I want to hug her and tell her I'm sorry, but the STOOPID part of my brain won't let me.

'YEAH! I'D BE BETTER OFF MY OWN!'

'FINE!' she roars. 'WELL, IF THAT'S HOW YOU FEEL, THEN MAYBE WE SHOULD SPLIT UP RIGHT NOW!'

'FINE BY ME!!'

'FINE!!!'

She steps backwards, on to the waiting train. My heart jumps into my throat.

'No, wait, Isha—'

But before I can say any more, the doors snap shut and the train pulls away.

TOON TOURIST INFORMATION

I can hardly breathe with WORRYPANIC.

What have I done?! Why did I say those things?! I watch the train chuntering off into the distance and feel like I'm falling fifty floors in a broken elevator.

'Everything all right, young man?'

I spin around to see a train guard, who happens to be a cartoon GIRAFFE, standing over me.

'Where does that train go to?' I yell up at her.

She squints at the disappearing train. **'Oh, that's the Runaway Train. It doesn't really have a destination – it just goes wherever its Artist feels like sending it.'**

'The *"Runaway Train"*?!' This answer does not do much to combat my WORRYPANIC.

'Yes indeedy,' the giraffe says. **'It might go on a nice sightseeing trip, or it might just plummet straight off the nearest cliff.'** She chuckles to herself. **'It's very unpredictable, the old Runaway Train.'**

As if to prove her point, the Runaway Train hops off the tracks and starts whizzing off in a totally different direction, until it's completely out of sight. My worrypanic levels are now OFF THE FLIPPING CHART. 'Well, do you know what time it'll get back?' I ask desperately.

The giraffe sighs. **'The whole concept of "time" doesn't really exist here in Toon World. I think it's probably because the clocks are all utter DOOFUSES. Take our main clock tower, for example . . .'** She cups her hands round her mouth and shouts up at the ginormous clock face watching over the whole station.

'Oi! Large Benjamin! How's things?'

The clock face breaks into a huge smile, and starts waving its arms around. 'Hello there, Sheryl! How are the kids? Oh, botheration! You made me move my arms. I can't remember what time I was on now . . .'

'You see?' Giraffe Guard Sheryl says. 'Clocks – absolute numpties.'

'But I need to find my friend!' I shout.

'Why don't you try Toon Tourist Information,' she suggests. 'They know everything – they'll sort you out.' She points down the platform with her ridonkulously long neck. 'It's just over there.'

'OK, thanks.'

'Before you go,' she says. 'Can I have a quick selfie with you? You're just so KOOKY looking!'

I sprint as fast as I can towards Tourist Information.

And even though I'm now getting used to seeing weird and wonderful Toons all around me, the Toon behind the info desk STILL makes me jump. Because . . . well, mainly because he has TWO HEADS.

The first head is super-smiley and friendly, but the second looks like it's chewing a mouthful of stinging nettles.

'**Hello!**' says Head Number One, beaming brightly. '**Welcome to Toon World! I'm Jonathan! How may I assist you with your trip today?**'

The other head just grunts and blows a raspberry at me.

'**Please ignore my evil twin, Ronathan,**' says Jonathan, his smile fading slightly. '**He doesn't share my passion for tourist information. However, I was the first one of us to find a job, so I'm afraid he just has to lump it.**'

'I wanted to be a traffic warden or a tax inspector,' says Ronathan sulkily. 'I HATE helping people. It goes against everything in the Evil Twin Code.'

'Please, Ronathan, not in front of a customer,' Jonathan hisses.

'Whatevs. I'm gonna listen to my heavy metal music.' Ronathan puts some earbuds in and starts violently head-banging.

Jonathan turns back to me, with his smile plastered on again. 'Sorry about that. Anyway, my strange-looking friend, how can I help you today?'

'I'm trying to find someone,' I say. 'She got on a train, and I don't know where it was going . . .'

'OK. What's her name?'

'Isha Kapesa. But she's not a Toon, you see. She's not from Toon World.'

'Ah.' Jonathan clicks his teeth with his tongue. 'I'm afraid I only have records for residents of Toon World. Do you happen to know anyone from Toon World?'

'Well . . .' And then it hits me. Obviously I DO know someone from Toon World. I know THREE people. 'Er,

do you maybe have an address for some Toons called . . .
Arley and Tapper and Jenny Weatherlegs?' I ask.

Jonathan starts tapping at the computer in front of
him. **'Arley, Tapper, Jenny Weatherlegs . . . Ah, here
we are! Yes, they live in Scrawlington Parkway. It's
not far. You can get there on the TTS.'**

'The TTS?'

**'Toon Transit System.
It's the tram on platform
number six.'**

'OK, brilliant,' I say.
'Thanks so much,
Jonathan. You've
been amazing.'

**'Oh, so you're
not gonna thank
ME, then?'** sneers
Ronathan, taking
out his earbuds. **'Have
I not been "amazing"
enough for you?'**

'Ronathan, seriously,' Jonathan snaps. 'Don't make me call Mum.'

'Oh, you wouldn't DARE call Mum!' his evil twin snaps back.

'Just try me, Ronathan! I'll call her! I'll call her

right now! And she will ground you so fast it'll make your head spin!'

'Well, we share the same body, Jonathan, so if I get grounded, so will you!'

'I don't mind! I'll happily take a grounding if it'll teach you not to meddle with my career!'

'Career! You call sitting in a booth all day talking to wet-wipes like this guy a "career" . . .'

I turn away from them, my mind focused only on Isha as I run towards the TTS.

CHAPTER TEN

THUNDERBOLTS AND LIGHTNING

'**S**crawlington Parkway!' the TTS announcer bellows. **'Next stop is Scrawlington Parkway!'**

The doors hiss open and I hop out, my heart still thump-thump-thumping as I think of Isha on that Runaway Train. I hear the giraffe guard's voice in my head again: **'It might just plummet off the nearest cliff . . .'**

Oh, **MONKEY NUTS.** If anything happens to Isha . . .

I take a deep breath and try to calm down. Arley and Tapper and Jenny will be able to help me find her. Surely they will.

But I need to find THEM first.

Scrawlington Parkway is loads less crowded than Toon Central Station, but I'm still getting weird looks and requests for selfies from every Toon I pass. There are posters stuck up all over the walls here too – on shops and houses and benches – all showing the same Toon on them.

Bill Dozer? Where have I heard that name? Oh yeah – the rabbit and tomato at the Arrivals Gate were talking about him. He's the new president of Toon World.

As I sprint past what must be the twentieth Bill Dozer poster in a row, I realize I actually have no idea which house is Arley and Tapper's! I'm about to hop back on the TTS and ask Jonathan for his help again, when I spot something. Above one of the houses there's a super-duper violent LIGHTNING STORM! Jet-black clouds with jagged bright yellow bolts shooting out of them.

Something clicks into place in my head . . .

Oh, MONKEY NUTS.

I jump over the house's fence into the back garden, and WALLOP – I come face to face with a scene that's very familiar . . . Because I drew it myself!

'GUYS!' I shout, over the crackle and rumble of thunderous lightning.

But they all stay exactly where they are – Jenny hovering in the air, shooting lightning out of her legs, as Arley and Tapper frazzle and fry below her. I see Arley's eyes swivel and clock me. Through clenched teeth, he hisses:

'F-F-F-FINN MORRIS! D-D-D-DIDN'T I TELL YOU N-N-N-NEVER TO LEAVE ONE OF OUR ADVENTURES UNF-F-F-INISHED AGAIN?!'

'Oh, MONKEY NUTS! ' I yell. The last time I left an Arley and Tapper comic unfinished, my poor characters ended up dangling off a bridge for ages, before being magicked into the

- 60 -

Real World! The only way I could put things right was by drawing the final frame of the comic . . .

But there's no way I can finish THIS comic – my sketchbook's still in my bedroom! I pat my pockets to see if I've at least got Kate Magenta's Magic Pen. But no – nothing there. Maybe Isha has it.

'F-F-F-F-FINNNNBOTT!!!' Tapper hisses, smoke billowing out of his ears as the lightning keeps frizzling him. 'CAN YOU P-P-P-PLEASE D-D-D-DO SOMETHING!!!!!'

'Er . . . I . . .' *What can I do?!* An idea thumps into my head. It's got to be worth a try.

THE END!

I shout, as loud as I can.

Arley →

The lightning bolts stop bursting out of Jenny Weatherlegs' trousers, and she drops straight back down to Earth. Arley and Tapper fall to the ground too, gasping in relief.

It worked!

'**I think,**' Arley says, holding up his burnt and frazzled frying pan, '**these eggs are now overdone.**'

I can't help laughing. Despite all the worrypanicful weirdness that's gone on this afternoon, it's so AMAZING to see these guys again!

'**Finntasmo!**' Tapper cries, jumping to his feet. '**What the absolute BLINKIN' FLIP are you doing in Toon World?!!**'

'**Yes, Finn Morris,**' Arley says, grinning. '**Kindly explain yourself.**'

'**You must be Finn,**' says Jenny Weatherlegs, walking towards me.

↑
Jenny
Weatherlegs

And even though she's definitely one of the *less* weird-looking Toons I've encountered so far today, it feels like a HUGE deal meeting her in person. I've already met Arley and Tapper in real life, but Jenny is Isha's character. We only started drawing her in our comics after we sent Arley and Tapper back home. Isha loves writing adventures for Jenny, and I know she puts bits of her own personality into her, just like I put bits of mine into Arley and Tapper.

Tapper

So, how's Jenny going to react when she finds out what I said to Isha? When she finds out I've LOST her Artist after we had a ginormous fight? She holds her hand up, and I feel like the slipperiest snake in the world as I high-five it.

Arley and Tapper pull me into a bear hug and ruffle

my hair. **'It's great to see you, Finn Morris,'** Arley says. **'But seriously – what are you doing here?'**

'How did you even get to Toon World?' Jenny asks.

'It's a long story,' I say. 'But basically, Zack Jellicoe came to find us—'

'Yorky's character?' Arley frowns.

'Who's Yorky?' says Jenny.

'Oh, he's literally the world's biggest numpty,' Tapper tells her. **'He used to be this super-famous cartoonist until he tried to steal me and Arley from Finnbot here.'**

'We busted him at Comic-Con,' Arley smirks, **'and he swore to wreak terrible vengeance on Finn Morris for destroying his career.'** He looks at me. **'Has he done that yet, by the way? The whole wreaking-terrible-vengeance-on-you thing?'**

'No,' I say, slightly nervously. 'No one's heard from him in months. It's like he's disappeared off the face of the Earth.'

'Hmm . . .' Arley rubs his chin thoughtfully. **'If I know**

bad guys – and I think I do – then he hasn't disappeared at all. He's simply holed up somewhere, plotting his dastardly revenge . . .'

'Or he might have gone on holiday, or something,' Tapper suggests cheerily. 'Cheeky fortnight at Center Parcs, maybe.'

'I think the dastardly revenge thing is more likely, Taps.'

'Ah well, whatever,' Tapper shrugs. 'We've already SNOT SHOTTED and TAIL SPINNED him once, we can easily do it again! Plus, we've got Lenny Jeatherwegs on our team now too!' He whacks Jenny Weatherlegs on the shoulder. 'I don't know if you know, Finnbot, but Jenny here can produce LITERALLY ANY KIND OF WEATHER out of her flippin' LEGS!'

'The clue's in my name,' says Jenny bashfully.

'Although it's not THAT impressive,' Tapper adds. 'I can also produce gale-force wind out of my trousers.'

'No, you CAN'T, Taps,' says Jenny.

'Can too! Observe . . .'

Tapper cocks up his leg and – PRRRRFFFTTT!!!!!! – lets out the most ear-rippingly loud FART ever. Jenny and Arley collapse on to the floor with laughter. Even I'm cracking up – until Jenny asks:

'So, Finn – where's Isha? Is she here in Toon World too? I'd LOVE to meet her!'

CHAPTER ELEVEN

TRUTH TIME

'**Y**eah, Finnbot, where's the Mighty Ishazar?'' Tapper says. 'You know we MUCH prefer her to you anyway!'

'**He's not wrong there,**' Arley nods. '**Isha Kapesa is a stone-cold LEGEND.**'

I feel myself turning red as they all smile at me. 'Well . . . we got zapped into Toon World together,' I begin. 'By this backfiring Magic Pen.'

Tapper sighs: '**Never meddle with Pajic Mens, Finnbot.**

That's, like, rule number ONE.'

I carry on. 'We nearly got squashed by a massive dinosaur, we chatted to a rabbit and a tomato, and then we found a big map of Toon World. But before we could decide where to go, I kind of . . . lost Isha.'

Jenny narrows her eyes at me. Arley and Tapper do the same.

'You . . . lost her?' Jenny says.

I gulp. Truth time. 'We had this massive row, you see. I told her I didn't care that she was moving to Los Angeles.'

'Wait - Los Angeles in AMERICA?' Tapper blurts.

'No, Taps, Los Angeles in Norwich,' Jenny sighs. And I'm reminded yet again just how similar Isha and I are to our characters.

'Since when is Isha Kapesa going to America?' Arley asks.

'It's been in the pipeline for a while, but it was only finalized two days ago,' Jenny says. 'Her dad's got a job over there.'

'How do YOU know that?' I ask her.

'She's my Artist,' Jenny shoots back. 'We've got a special connection.'

'Right, yeah,' Tapper nods. 'Like how Finnbot is my Artist, so I know that he secretly wears Peppa Pig underpants?'

'I do NOT!' I shout, remembering that I am literally wearing my Peppa pants at this very moment. I've had them since I was eight so they're a bit tight.

'Oi - stop laughing!'

I pull my trousers right up to my belly button to hide them.

'So, hang on, Finn Morris,' Arley says. 'Where exactly did you lose Isha?'

'At Toon Central Station,' I say. 'She just jumped on a train and it left.'

'Which train?' Jenny asks.

'The erm . . . Runaway Train?'

'WHAT??!' All three of them boggle their eyes at me. 'The Runaway Train is a dangerous RUFFIAN, Finn Morris!' Arley bellows. 'You never know WHERE that guy's gonna go!'

'I know! I know!' I shout back, as the worrypanic GRIPS me by the throat. 'Jenny – you said you've got a special connection with Isha. Can you tell where she is right now?'

'It's not that kind of connection,' Jenny snaps. 'I can't tell where she is. I can just sense how she's feeling. And right now -' she squeezes her eyes shut for a second, and then opens them – 'she's feeling SCARED.'

I feel a lump in my throat the size of a CRICKET BALL. Jenny throws me a look darker than the clouds she just conjured, and then stomps off.

Tapper puts his arm around me. 'Don't worry about J-Legs, Finnbot,' he says. 'She's just really angry at you because you've carelessly mislaid her beloved creator in a strange and terrifying new land. That's all.'

'Yeah, cheers, Tapper,' I say. 'Thanks for clearing

that up.'

'**No probs.**'

'You guys have to help me,' I plead. 'I can't let anything happen to Isha. There must be a way to stop that train, or at least find out where it's going!'

Arley steps forward and puffs his chest out, hero-style. '**Fear not, Finn Morris! Arley and Tapper would never let anything bad happen to the Mighty Isha Kapesa. Now, let's think about this. Who could stop the Runaway Train?**'

'**I'll tell you who!**' Tapper beams. '**Our new president!**'

'You mean Bill Dozer?' I say. 'There are posters for that guy everywhere.'

'**Yeah,**' Tapper says. '**He got elected as Toon World president the other day. Although I can't remember voting for him. Can you, Arl?**'

Arley shakes his spiky-haired head. '**Nope. We've never actually had a president in Toon World before – but apparently they're great. They look after everyone and make everything better.**'

'**This Dozer dude is in charge of the whole of Toon**

World - so he must be in charge of that pesky ol' Trunaway Rain too!' Tapper says.

'That's great.' For the first time in ages, I feel a glimmer of hope. 'But how do we find him?'

'He's giving a big speech later today,' Arley says. 'There's gonna be a MAHOOSIVE crowd - the whole of Toon World's gonna be there. Maybe if we can get there early, we can try to talk to him about Isha?'

'It's settled then!' Tapper shouts. 'We're all off to Number Ten Clowning Street!'

CHAPTER TWELVE

TAPPER'S TOUR OF TOON WORLD

Jenny Weatherlegs is STILL not speaking to me.

As the four of us make our way to Clowning Street on the TTS, she's barely said a single word. She won't even *look* at me. Although I'm pretty sure she is shooting bits of cold drizzle at me whenever I'm not looking.

I thought I couldn't feel more awful about what

happened with Isha – but this is making me feel TEN SQUILLION times worse.

The only thing that's giving me any hope is Arley's plan. If this Bill Dozer guy is in control of everything here, then surely he must be able to stop the Runaway Train? But then – Bill Dozer is the actual PRESIDENT of Toon World. We can't exactly just waltz right into his office . . . can we?

'Clowning Street!' the TTS driver announces. **'Alight here for Clowning Street! Home of the Toon Parliament!'**

We hop off, and the first thing I notice about this new area is that all the Toons look much more smart and professional around here. Even the traffic lights and

Trifle Tower

Lol-o-sseum

letterboxes are wearing suits and ties!

As we walk, Tapper points out some of the most famous sights of Toon World to me: **'Look, Finnbot – over there's the TRIFLE TOWER: two hundred metres high, and made en-flippin-tirely of jam, cream and sponge fingers! That's the LOL-O-SSEUM, it's an ancient sort of theatre type place that's been laughing out loud**

CelebriToon Village

for about two thousand years. No one knows why. Oh, and you see that posh-looking clump of swanky houses up on the hill? That's CelebriToon Village! All the famous cartoon characters live up there - the Simpsons, SpongeBob, the PAW Patrol pups. They don't mingle with us "common folk",' he adds sniffily. 'And over there-'

Jenny's voice interrupts him: 'Hey, you guys, look! We're here.'

CHAPTER THIRTEEN

NUMBER TEN CLOWNING STREET

She's right. We are.

The only problem is, there's an absolutely HUMUNG-O-RIFIC Toon policeman stood between us and the front door. And he does NOT look happy to see us.

Tapper strides up to him and sticks out his hand. **'Why, hello there, officer! Dovely lay, isn't it?'**

The policeman stares down at him like Taps is something he's picked out of his belly button.

Arley clears his throat. **'We're here to see President Bill Dozer,'** he announces, in a ridonkulous fake posh voice.

'Oh, are you indeed?' The policeman snorts with laughter. **'You think you can just rock up to Number Ten Clowning Street and be waved straight through to see El Presidente, do you?!'**

'That's certainly what we were hoping!' Tapper chimes.

'Well, it ain't the case, sunshine!' the policeman snaps. **'You think I just let any old Toon through this door? Not even the biggest celebrities in Toon World get to see the President! I had Peppa Pig on this doorstep yesterday, requesting a meeting with Mr Dozer. You've heard of Peppa Pig, haven't you?'**

'Course,' says Tapper. **'Finnbot's got her all over his undies.'**

'Shut up, Taps,' I hiss.

'Well, anyway, Mr Dozer said he was too busy to talk to her. I had to send Peppa Pig packing. So, I think the president has probably got better things to do than chinwag with the likes of YOU.'

Arley bristles and puffs his chest out. I can tell he's going into brave-possibly-bordering-on-stupid mode. 'Look here, officer!' he hollers. 'We demand – I repeat, DEMAND – to be let through that door! Unless you fancy a tangle with my legendary special move, the TAIL SPIN, and Tapper's bogey-blasting SNOT SHOT!'

'Cool it, Arl.' Jenny steps forward and gives the policeman a friendly smile. 'Sorry about my friend here. He gets a little overexcited. The thing is, we're here because one of our friends is in trouble. She's from the Real World, and she accidentally got on to the Runaway Train.'

The policeman raises his eyebrows. 'Oh, blimey. That guy is a dangerous RUFFIAN.'

'That's exactly what I said,' sniffs Arley.

'She could be in trouble,' Jenny continues. 'We were hoping we could speak to President Dozer and see if he would help us.'

'Hmm . . .' The policeman scratches his chin and eyes me suspiciously. 'And you're from the Real World too, are you?'

'That's right.'

'Hmm. I s'pose that's why you look so threedy-measurable, is it?'

'It is, yes.'

'Right.' I can tell the policeman is secretly quite impressed. 'You know,' he says, 'I reckon if I took a selfie with you I'd get at least fifty "likes" on Toonstagram. Maybe even sixty . . .'

'You can have as many selfies

with him as you want, as long as you let us in,' Jenny says.

The policeman frowns as he considers this. 'All right, it's a deal. Tell me your names, and I'll go and ask the big man if he wants to see you. Can't promise he will, though.'

Tapper punches the air with glee. 'Fantabuloso! I'm Tapper, that's Arley, that's Jenny Weatherlegs – AKA J-Legs AKA The Weather-Tron 3000 – and that threedy-measurable numpty is called Minn Forris. I mean: Finn Morris.'

The policeman nods and slams the door on us. But literally five seconds later, we hear his thumping footsteps again, and the door whips back open.

'Did you say your name was FINN MORRIS?!' he demands.

'Yes . . .'

He beckons us inside. 'Today's your lucky day . . .'

CHAPTER FOURTEEN

PRESIDENT DOZER

Number Ten Clowning Street is swanky.

I mean, SERIOUSLY swanky. You might even say it's abso-flippin-lutely SWANK-O-RIFIC.

There are giant glittering chandeliers hanging from the ceilings, and glinting golden candlesticks lined up on the fireplace. And obviously – since this is Toon World – all of them have faces and can talk . . .

'Tally ho, there!' coos one of the chandeliers in a voice posher than Prince William's. **'Welcome to Claaarning Street, ay hope you hev an epsolutely waaahhhhnderful visit!'**

'Er, cheers,' says Jenny.

The policeman leads us through to a mahoosive office, even swankier than the first room. In the middle of it is a GIGANTOMUNGOUS desk. And sat behind the desk is PRESIDENT BILL DOZER!

He stands up to greet us, smiling a bright twinkly smile. **'Hello there!'** he booms. **'How lovely to see you! I'm President Dozer!'**

He looked HUGE on the posters, but in real life he's like NINE SQUILLION times more so. The guy must be ten foot tall, and just as wide! He's wearing a super-smart James Bond-y kind of suit, and his gelled hair is so shiny I can practically see my FACE in it. He looms over us, offering his roast-chicken-sized hand to shake.

'So, you're FINN MORRIS from the Real World, are

you?' the president chuckles, as he pumps my hand so hard I'm worried my arm might come off. **'Well, it's a real, real PLEASURE to meet you!'**

'Er, thank you . . .'

He turns to Arley, Tapper and Jenny. **'And these must be your cartoon creations, eh?'**

'Yeah, they're—' I stop dead. 'Hang on – how did you know I'm a cartoonist?'

Dozer chuckles and swats the question away with his gigantic hand. **'Oh, just a lucky guess. You look like a very talented and creative young chap, that's all!'** He roars with laughter and ruffles my hair. I can't help grinning. That rabbit and tomato at the Arrivals Gate were right: he *does* seem like a pretty cool guy.

'Sit down, sit down, all of you,' he says, as a few Toon chairs scuttle underneath our bums to catch us. **'What can I get you? Would you like tea? Coffee? A ridiculously large bowl of Haribo Tangfastics?'**

'Ooh! I'll take the Tangfastics, please!' Tapper squeaks.

'Of course!' President Dozer claps his hands and a little table waddles in with a HUMUNGORIFIC bowl of sweets on it. Tapper plunges his hand in and starts munching away.

'Now, tell me,' says President Dozer. **'What can I do for you all?'**

'It's like this, El Presidente,' says Tapper, through a mouthful of Haribo. 'We've lost our great pal Isha Kapesa! She's from the Real World – just like Finnbot over there – and she jumped on to the Runaway Train by mistake!'

President Dozer gasps in horror. 'Oh, goodness me! The Runaway Train, you say?'

'Yes.' Jenny takes up the story, since Tapper's mouth is too stuffed with Tangfastics to continue. 'We were wondering if you could help us. We know the Runaway Train can't usually be controlled, but since you're the president and all, we thought maybe you could at least find out where it's going?'

President Dozer THUMPS the desk so hard it makes the whole floor shake. 'I'll do better than that! I'll send my own personal bodyguards out looking for it!'

'Wow – thank you!' says Jenny.

'This guy!' Tapper hoots. 'What a LEGEND!'

'Rick!' President Dozer calls. 'Can you come in here, please?'

The door opens and in walks a Toon who is even

MAHOOSIVER than President Dozer – but WAY less friendly-looking. In fact, he looks like someone's drawn a frowny-face emoji on a ROCK. He's wearing the same James Bond-y suit as President Dozer, but he looks a lot less comfy in it.

'This is my vice president,' Dozer says. 'Rick Ing-Ball.'

'How do, big man?' Tapper chimes. Rick just grunts at him.

'Rick, will you please send out a squadron of our guards to comb the whole of Toon World for the Runaway Train?' Dozer asks. 'There's a girl from the Real World on board, and it is VITAL that we find her and get her to safety.'

'Yes, boss,' Rick Ing-Ball grunts. 'Right away, boss.'

He walks back out, and Jenny turns to President Dozer. 'Thank you so much, Mr President.'

He grins his mega-watt grin at us. 'Don't mention it, Jenny. Now, if you four will excuse me, I've got some important presidential business to attend to . . .'

'That's probably code for needing a poo,' Tapper whispers in my ear. I giggle, but luckily I don't think President Dozer notices.

'I've got a big speech later today, and I need to practise for it,' he tells us. 'I'll be unveiling my vision for the future of Toon World!' Suddenly he claps his hands together. 'Tell you what – why don't you all stick around as my special guests? I'll make sure you get front row seats for my speech.'

'Wowza! That'd be awesome-pawesome!' says Tapper.

'And in the meantime, I'll get one of the candlesticks to give you the grand tour of Clowning Street.'

We all stand up to leave the room, and the chairs scuttle away from us. We may not have Isha back yet, but I feel much, MUCH better than I did ten minutes ago. 'Thank you again for your help,' I tell President Dozer. 'We really owe you one.'

'Think nothing of it, young man,' he beams. 'It's all in a day's work for the Toon World president. And don't you worry - we'll have your friend back, safe and sound, before you know it.' He scruffles my hair again and winks at me.

'That, Finn Morris, is a Bill Dozer promise.'

CHAPTER FIFTEEN

THE GRAND TOUR

'**H**onestly, what a GREAT guy!' Tapper gushes. 'I can't believe we've never had a president till now. They're awesome!'

'The Doze-Meister is indeed a flippin' good egg,' Arley agrees. 'I have no doubt that he will stop that Runaway Train and bring Isha Kapesa back to us!'

The four of us are following one of the Clowning

Street candlesticks as he gives us a guided tour of Number Ten. But, to be perfectly honest, the tour is INCRED-I-MENDOUSLY booooooring, so we're all just whispering among ourselves as the candlestick drones on ahead of us.

'He did seem pretty sure that he could help, didn't he?' says Jenny.

'Totes Malotes!' chirps Tapper. 'There's something about ol' Dozer that just fills you full of confidence, isn't there? He's clearly a dude who gets the job DONE!'

I smile. Because it's true. For the first time since Isha 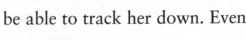 stepped on that train, my tummy doesn't feel TOTALLY squirmed up with worrypanic. President Dozer seemed so CERTAIN he'd be able to track her down. Even

Jenny looks a little bit brighter. She's stopped shooting bad weather at me, anyway.

'And I'll tell you another thing,' Tapper says. 'We–'

'AH-HEM!' The candlestick is staring at us, with an annoyed look on its face. 'If you'd KINDLY pay attention to my guided tour?'

'Oh, sorry, dude,' Tapper says. 'Crack on.'

'Right,' huffs the candlestick. 'I was saying that this

particular staircase was first drawn back in 1791 by an artist named Leonardo de Baxendale. There's a rather amusing anecdote about the pencil he used to sketch it . . .'

Arley and Tapper sigh and trudge along after him, leaving Jenny and me walking behind. She's still not looking at me. I feel awkward suddenly.

'I really am sorry, Jenny,' I whisper. 'I feel like this is all my fault.'

'Yeah, well,' she mutters. 'Isha did warn you about that Magic Pen.'

I flinch. 'How do you know about that?'

'I told you,' she says. 'She's my Artist. We've got a special connection. It's like . . . it's like sometimes I can see into her head. I know what she's thinking.'

'I feel like that too!' I say. 'Like we can read each other's minds!' But the excitement quickly fades as I remember that Isha is out there somewhere, scared and alone, aboard the wild and dangerous Runaway Train. 'Or at least, I *used* to feel like that . . .'

Jenny finally pulls her gaze away from the window

and turns to look at me. But her brown eyes don't look angry or annoyed, like I'm expecting them to. They just look sad.

'You know she feels the same way, right?'

I blink. 'What?'

'She feels the way you feel. That you two are such close friends you can sometimes read each other's thoughts. You're the best friend she's ever had, Finn.'

I feel my face going red as confusion and guilt and happiness and sadness all headbutt each other inside me. 'No, I'm not, Jenny,' I say. 'Trust me.'

'What makes you think that?'

I shrug. 'If I was the best friend she ever had, then she wouldn't be leaving, would she?'

Jenny clicks her tongue against her teeth, annoyed. 'You think she WANTS to go to America?'

'Well . . . yeah.'

She slaps her palm against her forehead. 'Ugh, you're such a DOOFUS, Finn. She's TERRIFIED of moving! She's terrified of being uprooted from the place she grew up in, she's terrified of moving to a whole new school.

But most of all she's terrified of losing her best friend and cartoon co-creator . . . YOU.'

I try to speak, but I can't. Jenny seems to understand. She puts her hand on my shoulder.

'Finn. It's OK. You had a fight. You'll make up and be friends again.'

I shake my head. 'We won't. You should have heard the things I said to her. She'll never want to speak to me again. I told her I'd be glad if we weren't friends any more. I told her I was happier making comics on my own.'

Jenny looks away, and it's like the shame I was already feeling has been shoved under a GARGANTUOUS magnifying glass. I swallow hard because I can feel the tears trying to come.

'I didn't mean any of it,' I tell her. 'I was just hurt and scared about her leaving me.'

Jenny sighs and nods. 'She'll understand, Finn. I promise you. We just need to find her so you can explain.' She must see how utterly miseri-fied I am, because she gives me a smile and punches me softly on the arm. **'Look, I'm just a cartoon schoolgirl who - for some reason no one's quite sure of - can shoot weather out of her legs. What do I know about anything? But something tells me that you and Isha are meant to stay best friends. You're meant to make comics together. And I don't think even putting the whole Atlantic Ocean between you can stop that.'**

I bite the inside of my cheek hard. The tears are trying to come again now – but this time there are happy ones intermingled with the sad ones. My heart is badump-dump-dumping in my chest. I *have* to find Isha. I have to say sorry. I have to FIGHT to win back my best friend!

I'm about to tell Jenny exactly that when suddenly – KA-BLOOOOM!!! – there's an almighty EXPLOSION outside. It's so loud that it makes the walls shudder.

'What was that?!' Jenny peers out of the window next to us. Outside in the presidential gardens, we see whizzing and banging

SPARKS shooting over a ginormous pile of cartoon rubble – like a wall has just been knocked down.

But we can't see WHO knocked it down, because the curtain is suddenly whipped across the window. 'Excuse me!' snaps the candlestick.

'What just happened down there?' Jenny asks.

'That's none of your concern,' huffs the candlestick. **'Now, if you'd like to follow me to the dining room, we have prepared a light luncheon for you . . .'**

CHAPTER SIXTEEN

JENNY THE GENIUS

'**OH, SWEET LORD NUNKEY MUTS!**' Tapper exclaims, as he looks around him. '**If this is a LIGHT lunch, then I'd love to see a HEAVY one!**'

The candlestick has just showed us into the mega-swish presidential dining room, where the main table is absolutely HEAVING with delici-o-rific goodies. Plates of piping hot sausage and mash; thick cheesy-drippin' slices of pepperoni pizza; mahoosive slabs of custard-

and-cream-slathered choccie cake – there's enough here to feed a whole ARMY!

The only problem is – all of it is toody-measurable.

I mean, two dimensional.

'I'm not sure I can eat this,' I say, nibbling a slice of pizza that tastes strangely like paper and ink.

'Great news!' Tapper squeals. **'More for the rest of us!'**

'If you'll kindly wait here until President Dozer's speech,' the candlestick says, **'I shall come and fetch you then.'**

'Can do, candle dude!' Tapper quips, nine sausages already stuffed into his gob.

'Hmm. Yes,' the candle says stuffily, before stomping back out and closing the door.

'Right, let's chow down,' Arley says, diving head first into the feast with Tapper. But Jenny's still peering out of the window into the garden. **'What was that noise?'** she mutters. **'It looked like something . . . blew up outside.'**

I nod. 'Yeah. That was kind of strange. Since I can't

actually eat any of this stuff, maybe I'll go out and have a look . . .'

I try the door. But it's locked.

'That's weird.'

'**Very weird,**' Jenny agrees.

'**If you guys don't hurry up, I'm gonna finish the chocolate Hobnobs!**' Tapper calls. '**Oh, wait - too late.**'

Jenny's not listening. She tries opening the window, but she can't.

'Don't tell me that's locked too?' I ask.

'**Yeah.**' She frowns. '**Something's not right here. And we're gonna find out what it is.**'

Arley pushes an entire roast chicken into his mouth and strains as he tries to swallow it. '**Whash "not right",**' he gulps between bites, '**ish you two misshing out on all this delissshous grub.**'

'How are we going to find out what that explosion was if we're locked in?' I ask Jenny.

Her frown melts slowly into a smile. '**The thing about locks, Finn, is that they break when they get really** cold . . .' She lifts one leg up and aims it at the big bulky window lock. **'The forecast for this afternoon: freezing rain . . .'**

As soon as the rain hits the lock, it freezes solid. We can hear it creaking and groaning as the ice ripples through it. **'Just one little tap should do it,'** Jenny says. She knocks the lock gently with her knuckles, and – CRACCKKKKKKKK!! – it shatters into a million little pieces!

'You are a genius, Jenny!' I laugh.

'Hey, I can't take credit for that idea,' she shrugs. **'Isha came up with it. She's been planning to use it in one of your comics for a while.'**

A feeling swims through me – I can't tell if it's a happy one or a sad one. Oh man, I hope President Dozer can stop that train before it's too late . . .

Jenny pushes the window open and looks at Arley and Tapper. **'Come on, you two.'**

'You go ahead without us,' Tapper says, tipping an entire bowl of Maltesers down his throat.

'NOW!' Jenny shouts.

They both leap up from their chairs. **'Yes, Miss Weatherlegs!'**

All four of us hop out of the window and into the garden. Jenny leads the way across the lawn, until we see the pile of Toon rubble, which is being cleared away by a few other candlesticks. Stood behind the pile are President Dozer and Rick Ing-Ball. They're huddled together, whispering. We can't hear what they're saying. Dozer is smiling, as usual, but his smile is different than it was before. My mum always says that you can tell when someone's really smiling if they smile with their eyes as well as their mouth. And right now Bill Dozer's mouth is smiling – but his eyes definitely aren't.

'There's El Presidente!' Tapper says. **'Let's go and ask him what happened!'**

Jenny holds him back, guiding the four of us behind a tall hedge. **'Hang on, Taps. Something about this feels ... wrong.'**

'I wonder what they're saying,' I mutter, as we stare through the leaves.

Jenny thinks for a second and then a grin spreads

across her face. **'I know how we can find out . . .'**

She leaps up into the air, and suddenly the whole garden is filled with some sort of thick, grey smoke. No, wait – not smoke. FOG. I glance up to see billowing clouds of it seeping out of the bottom of Jenny's trousers! Within seconds, I can hardly see any further than my own hands.

'Classic J-Legs,' Tapper chuckles.

I feel her drop back on to the grass beside me, and grab my arm. **'Let's go,'** she whispers.

We feel our way through the mist, until we can hear voices. Bill Dozer and Rick Ing-Ball's voices . . . We must be two metres away from them, but they can't see us through the clouds of fog!

'Strange weather,' we hear Bill Dozer say. **'I've never seen mist this thick before.'**

'I don't like it, boss,' says Rick Ing-Ball, sounding worried. **'The weather forecast said sun all day. It didn't say anything about fog so thick you couldn't even see your own nose. Something fishy's going on here . . .'**

Dozer snorts. **'Oh, come off it, Rick! Stop being so ruddy paranoid! Now, let's get back to discussing the finer details of our dastardly evil plan . . .'**

Jenny grips my arm tight.

'Did he say "dastardly evil plan"?' Arley hisses.

My blood turns cold.

'Surely not!' Tapper whispers. **'We must've misheard. Dozer is a Grade-A classic lad.'**

'Shhhh,' Jenny urges, and we all strain our ears to listen.

'So, the test run worked perfectly,' Dozer says. 'We successfully smashed that wall to pieces, which means the rest of Toon World can be smashed to pieces too. This place CAN be destroyed ... Once we've got everyone in this ridiculous dimension gathered together for my big victory speech, we'll jump straight into action. Just remember, Rick: wait until my signal before you transform. OK?'

'OK, boss.'

I hear Jenny whisper: 'Transform? Into what?'

'We'll put Finn Morris and his silly little sidekicks in the front row, so they'll be the first ones to feel the full POWER of my speech!'

'Very good, boss.'

'Silly little what now?!' Tapper hisses.

'Now - any word on the Kapesa girl?' Dozer asks.

Jenny's grip on my arm gets even tighter. My heart's beating so loudly I'm worried they'll hear it. What is happening here?!

'Nothing yet, boss,' says Rick Ing-Ball. 'I've told our

guards to be on the lookout for the Runaway Train. If anyone spots it, they'll bring the Real World girl back here, and we'll sit her right next to Finn Morris in the front row, so she can enjoy the fireworks. If not, that stupid train will probably run itself off a cliff, taking the Kapesa girl with it.'

Dozer laughs. 'Ha-ha! Excellent. What an unexpected pleasure - the chance to wipe Toon World off the face of this Earth, AND teach those two meddling little fools a lesson as well! I think this calls for a villainous cackle. Won't you join me, Rick?'

'Love to, boss.'

'Muwaha-ha-ha-ha!!'

'Muuu-wa-ha-ha-ha-ha!!!!'

'MUUUU-WA-HA-HA-HA-HAAAAAA!!!'

'What . . . What is happening?' I can feel Tapper trembling next to me. I'm shaking too. My head is spinning and terror is pounding through my chest like a million panicked ELEPHANTS. I thought we could trust these two. I thought they were going to bring Isha back to safety. And now I find out they want to—

'"Wipe Toon World off the face of this Earth"?' Arley seethes. 'Those villainous, double-crossing NUMPTIES! Time for our special moves, Taps . . .'

But Jenny is way ahead of him. I feel her let go of my arm, and a second later, I hear her voice – loud, clear and EXTREEEEEMELY angry . . .

'Oi, Dozer! Oi, Ing-Ball!' she yells through the fog. 'Here's something else the weather forecast didn't predict!'

Out of nowhere, two MAHOOOOSIVE white hailstones – each the size of a basketball – slice through the fog and THWACK Dozer and Ing-Ball right in the face! I see them tumble to the ground in a dazed heap, and then Jenny's panicked eyes emerge through the fog.

'Guys, I think now would be an excellent time to RUN!'

CHAPTER SEVENTEEN

CLOUDBUSTING

I sprint as fast as I can through the fog, my heart going SIX SQUILLION miles a minute.

I hope hope HOPE I'm following Jenny, but the mist is still so thick that I can't see a single thing. I'm just running and running and RUNNING into an endless grey cloud. I look back behind me. I've lost Arley and Tapper too!

'Jenny?' I call. 'Arley?! Tapp—'

KA-SMACKKKKK!!!!

I hit something. Or *someone*.

I run into them so hard that I'm knocked straight back on to my bum. I look up in panic, and see a grinning head poking through the fog, with a black wick sticking out of the top . . .

'**I told you,**' the candlestick says, '**to wait in the dining room.**'

'**Unhand us!**' Arley shouts. '**Unhand us right this second, you waxy little wrong'uns!!**'

The four candlesticks that have marched us all back into Number Ten cackle with horrid laughter as they bundle us into a tiny cramped basement room with BARS on the windows.

'**Stay in there and keep quiet!**' one of them smirks, before slamming the door.

'**Maybe we SHOULD have stayed in the dining room,**' Tapper sighs. '**At least they had Hobnobs in there.**'

Arley jumps to his feet and starts

pacing our prison cell. **'So Dozer and Ing-Ball are BAD GUYS, are they?!'** he hollers. **'Well, here's a newsflash: Arley and Tapper eat bad guys for BREAKFAST!'**

'Actually, I eat Honey Nut Cheerios for breakfast,' Tapper says. **'They're dee-flippin-lectable – and a good source of fibre to boot.'**

'IT'S A METAPHOR, TAPS! I'M BEING METAPHORICAL!'

'Oh, OK. Gotcha.'

'Finn.' Jenny looks at me, her eyes wide with panic. **'What are we gonna do?'**

I know what she's thinking, because I'm thinking the exact same thing: *we need to get to Isha before Bill Dozer does.*

Right on cue, the door swings open and the Toon president comes STORMING in. His barrel-like body practically fills the whole of this tiny room. There's a big red bump on his noggin where Jenny's hailstone thwacked him. Serves him RIGHT.

'You just couldn't play nicely, could you?' he sneers at us.

'Dozer!' Arley yells back. 'So you're a BAD GUY, are you? Well, you should know that Arley and Tapper eat bad guys for BREAKFAST!'

'Yeah!' Tapper shouts. 'And we mean that feta-morically! Because we actually eat HONEY NUT CHEERIOS!'

'LET ME DO THE TALKING, TAPS!!'

'SORRY!!!!'

ENOUGH!

Dozer booms. His voice is so loud that the bars on the window rattle. 'I thought we could do this the easy way,' he says. 'I thought I could give you the best seats in the house at my victory parade, so you could watch the fireworks. But no. You just HAD to make trouble.'

'We weren't making trouble – we were overhearing your EVIL plan,' Jenny fires back.

'We won't let you wipe Toon World off the face of the Earth!' I yell.

'You'll have a hard time stopping me when you're locked in this room.' He jabs a hot-dog-sausage-sized finger at Jenny. 'And as for you, Miss Weatherlegs, the door outside is swarming with guards – if they hear a single rumble of thunder, or crackle of lightning, or hiss of fog from your magical toes, then they'll be straight in here to wallop you all with something a little harder than a hailstone. Is that clear?'

'Why are you doing this?' Jenny shouts at him. 'What have you got against us? What have you got against Toon World?'

'All will be explained later,' he smirks. 'Right now, I've got a victory speech to give. Outside this building, the good citizens of Toon World are assembling to see their beloved new president speak. And they have no idea what I've got in store for them . . .' He cackles a horrible cackle. 'Once I've finished with them, I'll be back to deal with you four.'

'You won't get away with this, Dozer!' Arley hollers. But it's too late – he's already slammed the door behind him.

CHAPTER EIGHTEEN

TEAM MEETING

Tapper presses his eye to the keyhole.

'Yep, he wasn't lying. There are guards GALORE out there. We wouldn't stand a chance against them all. Even with all our meshal spooves.'

'What are we going to do?' I moan. 'Something terrible's going to happen at that victory speech, and we won't be there to stop it. And Isha's out there somewhere too, and we can't save her either!'

Arley grabs me by my shoulders and starts shaking me. **'Get a hold of yourself, Finn Morris! Now is not the time for panic!'**

Tapper jumps over and starts shaking me as well. **'Yeah, Finnbot, get a hold of yourself! FOR THE LOVE OF NUNKEY MUTS, GET A HOLD OF YOURSELF!'**

I'm juddering like a jelly in a tumble dryer on top of a bouncy castle. 'G-G-G-GUYS, C-C-CAN Y-Y-YOU P-P-PLEASE S-S-TOP S-SHAKING M-M-ME?!'

'Oh yeah, sorry,' Tapper says. **'Got a bit carried away.'**

I flop down on to the hard wooden bench, and Arley steps forward. **'OK, now that Finn Morris has got a hold on himself, I propose a team meeting where we will discuss how we can get ourselves out of this particular pickle. All in favour?'**

'Just get on with it, Arl,' Jenny snaps.

Arley nods. **'OK: team meeting in session. Arley presiding. First item on the agenda: how do we get ourselves out of this particular pickle. I'm throwing** the question open to the floor – any thoughts?'

'Well, I've got one idea,' Jenny says. 'It's a long shot, but–' She kicks up her leg and aims it at the tiny barred window.

'No, Jenny!' I hiss. 'You heard what Dozer said: if the guards hear you conjuring lightning and thunder, they'll come straight in!'

'Don't worry, Finn,' she says, calmly. 'This particular weather is completely silent . . .'

She squeezes her eyes shut, and then suddenly . . . a HUMONGOUS, GLITTERING RAINBOW shoots out from her left trouser leg!

'**Wowzers.**' Tapper stares wide-eyed at the stupendous multi-coloured arch stretching into the distance. It reminds me of something – but right now I can't put my finger on what.

'**That's bee-yoo-tiful, J-Legs. But how exactly is it gonna help us escape?**'

'**Maybe it won't,**' Jenny says. '**We'll see . . .**'

Arley wrinkles his forehead, confused. '**O . . . kay. So, Jenny's kicked us off by shooting a rainbow out of her legs. Interesting start. Any other thoughts?**'

Tapper's hand shoots into the air. **'Ooh! Ooh! Me! Pick me!'**

'That AREN'T about Hobnobs,' Arley adds.

Tapper puts his hand down.

Arley sighs and turns to me. **'Finn Morris - you're up. Any bright ideas?'**

I close my eyes and rack my brains. I HAVE to think of an idea. We HAVE to find a way out. We HAVE to find Isha. We HAVE to stop Bill Dozer! We can't let him destroy this brilliant 'n' bananas, wild 'n' wacky dimension where EVERYTHING is alive – the lamp posts, the cars, the candles, the—

Hang on.

I open my eyes as an idea starts to form vaguely in my head. 'Hey, you guys . . .' I say. 'Pretty much everything is ALIVE in Toon World, right?'

'Yes-a-rooney,' Tapper nods. **'In**

fact, that's our national motto: "Toon World: Pretty Much Everything Is Alive Here".'

I walk slowly towards the thick brick wall. 'So, if everything's alive, then . . .' I reach up and tap one of the hard red bricks in the wall. 'Erm . . . Hello?'

Nothing. **MONKEY NUTS.**

But then . . .

An EYE appears, BLINKING, in the middle of the brick! I almost jump out of my skin with shock and delight!

'Mmmph. I was sleeping,' the brick mumbles. **'Whaddayou want?'**

I gulp: 'Erm . . . Sorry to bother you. We were just wondering if you and your friends would be so kind as to . . . move for a few seconds, so we can escape?'

The brick yawns loudly, and its eye swivels to look at me. **'Blimey. You're quite weird-looking, aren't you?'**

'Yes, I'm, erm, from the Real World.'

'Oh aye? I've got a cousin who lives there. He's

part of that Westminster Abbey building. Hey – can I get a selfie with you?'

A *brick* is asking me for a selfie. I pinch myself quickly just to check this is definitely NOT a dream. Nope: it's really happening.

'Yes. Of course,' I tell the brick. 'If you and your friends would just shift sideways slightly so we can get out, you can take a selfie with me.'

'All right, then. OI, LADS!' the brick shouts. 'Shift sideways, will you?'

There is a loud groan, and suddenly EVERY BRICK

IN THE WALL has its eyes open! A few of them wriggle sideways and suddenly the tiny room floods with light.

'I . . . **can't believe it,'** Arley whispers, staring out into Toon World.

'**Me neither** . . .' Tapper says.

'**Finn Morris actually had a GOOD idea!'**

I burst out laughing, as Jenny throws her arms around me. '**Too right, he did! Nice one, Finn! Now, let's get out of here!'**

CHAPTER NINETEEN

TURN BACK NOW!

We step through the wall of talking bricks – after I've taken a few selfies with them. It immediately closes back up behind us, and that's when we come face to face with the most MAHOOSIVE crowd I've ever seen.

Toons of all shapes and sizes are hurrying past, and the air is full of laughter and excited chatter.

'They're all going to Dozer's victory speech,' Jenny hisses.

'Not if we can help it!' Tapper cries. 'Arl, give me a boost!'

He leaps on to Arley's shoulders, wobbles to get his balance, and then starts shouting at the top of his voice:

'STOP! EVERYONE! STAY AWAY FROM THE VICTORY SPEECH! RETURN TO YOUR HOMES AND PLACES OF BUSINESSES!'

A passing caterpillar slithers by, and looks up at Tapper. 'Not likely, mate - we all want to see President Dozer unveil his new plan for Toon World.'

'Yeah,' adds a gorilla, stomping along after him. 'Plus Dozer has promised every Toon who turns up a free packet of chocolate Hobnobs.'

PRESIDENT BILL DOZER WANTS YOU!

'Ooh, has he really?' Tapper squeaks. 'Well, fair enough, then - crack on!'

'TAPPER!' Jenny shouts.

TO ATTEND HIS VICTORY SPEECH ABOUT THE FUTURE OF TOON WORLD!

'Sorry, J-Legs, sorry.'

Now it's Jenny's turn to speak to the crowd. She starts flapping her hands about to get people's attention. **'Something bad is going to happen at this speech!'** Jenny yells. **'Please, everyone needs to turn back NOW!'**

But no one's listening to her. They're just shoving past, completely ignoring us, as they hurry towards the huge stage that's been set up at the end of Clowning Street. There's a MEGA-SIZED banner hanging over it that says: PRESIDENT BILL DOZER – A BRIGHT NEW FUTURE FOR TOON WORLD. Behind is a HUUUUUGE photo of Dozer's grinning face.

Arley helps Tapper down from his shoulders. **'They're not listening,'** he snaps. **'Come on, we need to get to the front!'**

I follow the three of them as they start trying to push through the crowd towards the stage. As I look up at a flock of Toon parrots flapping over us, I see Jenny's rainbow still stretching far, far, FAR into the distance.

Tapper's right: it *is* beautiful. But it isn't much help . . .

No time to think about that now. Arley and Jenny

are leading the way, barging through the thick crowd of Toons. But we're hardly moving. It's also not helping that every single person we pass is trying to get me to take a selfie with them.

'Please, move out of our way!' I shout. 'This is important!'

But the crowd is just getting denser and denser. Finally, we hit a complete block. A wall of Toons that stretches right up to the stage. I literally cannot move a muscle!

'**Jenny!**' Arley shouts. '**How about hitting that stage with a rainstorm or some lightning?**'

'**I can't, I'm totally stuck!**' Jenny yells back. '**I can't even move my legs to shoot weather out of them!**'

The noise around us gets louder and louder. I squint at the stage. Someone has walked up on to it. Someone who must be ten foot tall and just as wide. He gets to the podium, and waves his hand for silence. A hush comes over the whole crowd.

Bill Dozer is about to speak.

CHAPTER TWENTY

THE VICTORY SPEECH

'Friends, Toons, Countrymen!' cries Bill Dozer. 'I come before you as your glorious, bounteous and incredibly good-looking leader!'

A massive roaring cheer goes up from the crowd. Next to me, Tapper tuts loudly. '**Not exactly modest, this dude, is he?**'

'**You have elected me your President,**' Dozer announces, '**and I am here to say one thing: YOU WILL NOT REGRET IT!**'

Another ear-busting cheer goes up. Everywhere I look, I see smiling Toon faces, beaming towards their new leader. And none of them has any idea that something utterly butterly HORRIFIC is about to happen.

But *what*?!

I feel the worrypanic surging inside me. I try to wriggle free, but I'm blocked in by Toons on all sides. How are we supposed to stop this when we can't even move?! I can tell Arley, Tapper and Jenny are all thinking the same thing. They're looking around desperately for a way to the stage. But there isn't one.

Rick Ing-Ball is up there now too, stood just behind Dozer, with a nasty smirk on his boulder-like face.

Dozer slicks back his oily quiff and keeps talking.

'I was elected your president on a solemn vow – that I would change Toon World for the better!'

Another cheer. Although a few people around us are murmuring, 'I quite like it the way it is!' and, 'You know, I don't actually remember voting for him . . .'

'And you know what I think?' Dozer pulls the microphone off its stand and walks towards the front of the stage, his nasty grin getting wider and wider. 'I think it would be much, much BETTER if Toon World . . . didn't exist at all!'

A few people cheer automatically, then stop. The whole crowd is suddenly engulfed in confused silence. People start whispering, 'WHAT did he just say?'

Jenny shoots me a terrified look that says: 'Here we go . . .'

'That's right!' Dozer carries on.

I THINK TOON WORLD IS A RUBBISH PLACE, FULL OF RUBBISH TOONS...

AND I WILL NOT REST UNTIL IT IS WIPED OFF THE FACE OF THE EARTH!

My heart is GALLOPING like a ten-legged horse in the Olympic 100 metres. Around us, the befuddled muttering is turning to angry shouting, as thousands of Toons start to boo and jeer:

'How dare you?!'

'You take that back!'

'Does this mean there's no chocolate Hobnobs?'

Bill Dozer turns to Rick Ing-Ball, his evil grin now so wide it nearly splits his face in half. **'Rick – on my signal . . . Three, two, one . . . NOW!'**

And then the two of them . . . *change*.

CHAPTER TWENTY-ONE

OHHHHHH, NOW I GET IT!

The two baddies SOAR up to thirty, forty, fifty times their original height, as their bodies click and clank and whirr mechanically!

Dozer's legs buckle inwards and become GIANT METAL WHEELS. His mouth becomes a glinting metal BLADE the size of a tennis net, and through his razor-sharp teeth he laughs the loudest and most GHASTLY laugh you've ever heard. Next to him, Rick Ing-Ball's body morphs into a monstrous chugging TANK. His head swings loose on a long chain, swirling and swooping over the screaming crowd. Sparks fly from them as they tower over us like evil mountains . . .

'Ohhhhh,' says Tapper, as CHAOS breaks loose around us. 'Now I get it! Bill Dozer - like Bulldozer - and Rick Ing-Ball, like Wrecking Ball! We should've spotted that, really, shouldn't we, guys?'

Around us, twenty thousand terrified Toons are screeching and running in horror as Dozer and Ing-Ball change into nightmarish MACHINES before our eyes!

Dozer's voice is so loud it makes my teeth shake. 'Now I shall wreak my revenge on Toon World! Rick - let's flatten this puny dimension once and for all!'

The two skyscraper-sized wrong'uns whirr into action. Bill ploughs into a huge row of buildings, smashing them to smithereens, and Rick starts swinging his ghastly metal head at any Toon in reach.

I'm so scared I can barely stand up. But then I feel Arley grip my shoulder. 'We have to do something!' he cries.

Some of his bravery must rub off on me, because I take a deep breath, and nod. 'What's the plan?'

'Finn,' he says, 'you get as many Toons to safety as you can. Taps, Jenny: follow my lead - it's time to send these mean machines to the scrap heap!'

Arley's black tail starts whirring like a helicopter blade. 'TAIL SPIN!!' he yells, as he ZIPS into the air, towards Bill Dozer!

Tapper presses a finger to his humungous nose. 'SNOT SHOT!!!' he bellows. And – SQUELLLLCHHHHH – he shoots a watermelon-sized bogey at Rick Ing-Ball's swinging face.

Jenny flashes me a smile. 'Good luck, Finn.' Before I can tell her the same, she soars up into the air, yellow SHEETS OF LIGHTNING sparking from her legs!

I want to help them, but I know full well that I can't shoot electric weather out of my feet, or fly through the air, or blast ballooning bogies out of my schnozz. There's only one thing I can do.

I take a deep breath and at the top of my voice I shout, 'Who wants a selfie?'

CHAPTER TWENTY-TWO

A PLACE TO HIDE

By the time I've turned the corner of Clowning Street, I must have two hundred Toon Worlders sprinting behind me. I've no idea whether they trust me to get them to safety or if they really just want a selfie.

Because the truth is: I have absolutely NO CLUE where I'm going.

My eyes are darting frantically left and right as I run. We need a place to hide. Somewhere Bill Dozer

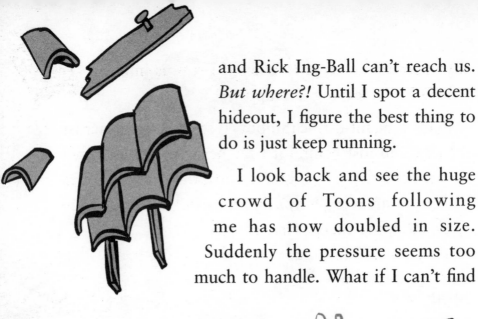

and Rick Ing-Ball can't reach us. *But where?!* Until I spot a decent hideout, I figure the best thing to do is just keep running.

I look back and see the huge crowd of Toons following me has now doubled in size. Suddenly the pressure seems too much to handle. What if I can't find

anywhere for us to go?! What if I run us into a DEAD END, leaving us trapped?!

Jenny's gigant-o-rific rainbow is still zigzagged across the sky, and just behind it I see her, Arley and Tapper flying about, doing their best to battle the two mega-sized bad guys. But even Jenny's lightning storm doesn't seem to be stopping them. They're still tearing down buildings and ripping up roads.

What if they CAN'T be defeated? What if—

'Oi! Watch where you're going!'

I skid round another corner and come face to face with a

very angry alien head scowling at me. And right next to it, an identical alien head – although this one's much friendlier.

'Jonathan!' I cry. 'Ronathan!'

'Ah – you're the young chap from the Real World,' Jonathan beams. **'How are you enjoying your visit to Toon World so far?'**

We all duck as a tower block comes sailing through the air above us.

'It's . . . eventful,' I say.

Jonathan frowns. **'I do apologize for all this rampaging mayhem and destruction – this is NOT the image we at the Toon World Tourist Information would wish to promote.'**

Ronathan snorts. **'It's EXACTLY the sort of image I'd wish to promote.'**

'Will you stick a cork in it, Ronathan?'

'I'll stick a cork in YOU, Jonathan.'

'Oh, grow up . . .'

I am very aware of the big-and-getting-bigger crowd of terrified Toons at my back. 'Guys, listen – can you stop bickering for ONE SECOND? I need a safe place for us all to hide out. Can you think of anywhere?'

Jonathan's face brightens. **'You're asking the right chap here! As the Senior Tourist Management Officer for Toon World, I know every single nook and cranny of this dimension.'** Ronathan rolls his eyes and makes puking sounds. Jonathan starts tapping his chin thoughtfully. **'Now, let me see . . . A good hiding place . . .'**

Behind us, there's the sound of RRRR-RIPPING concrete and another tower block comes whizzing over our heads.

'Maybe think a bit quicker?' I suggest.

Jonathan screws his face up in concentration. **'Sorry – I'm racking my brains but I can't think of anywhere thousands of Toons could hide out in safety . . .'**

Ronathan makes a frustrated grunting sound. **'Well, what about down in the sewers?'** he snaps, nodding at a manhole cover by my feet. **'There's tons of space down there, and that hole is way too small for Bill Dozer to get through.'**

'The sewers!' I shout. 'That's BRILLIANT!'

Jonathan is staring at his evil twin in awestruck amazement. **'Ronathan . . . you've just saved the day!'**

Ronathan goes red and shrugs. **'I . . . er . . . don't know about that. It was just a suggestion.'**

'Well, you should make MORE suggestions!'

'Well, maybe I would if you'd let me,' Ronathan says shyly. **'You're not the only one**

who has a passion for Toon tourist information, you know.'

'I thought you HATED Toon tourist information!'

'No, I don't. I've always loved it. I'm just not as confident as you, so I never spoke up.'

'Oh, Ronathan! Let's never fight again!'

For the first time, an ACTUAL smile spreads across Ronathan's face. **'Oh, brother!'** he cries. **'Come here and give me a cuddle!'**

The twins hug. Which – since they share the same body and arms – looks quite weird, to be honest.

I turn to the crowd of scared Toons behind me. 'Everybody – down in the sewers, NOW!'

Jonathan/Ronathan yanks open the manhole and starts ushering Toons down the ladder.

'Great work, you guys,' I tell them. 'You get everybody down there – I'm going back for anyone we might have missed.'

'OK! Ronathan – let's go!'

'You got it, Jonathan!'

I sprint back towards Clowning Street, sending any Toons I see straight to the sewers. Every building I pass is smashed or crushed or crumbling. On the horizon is the looming figure of Rick Ing-Ball. I can still see Arley, Tapper and Jenny, in the air and on the ground, throwing everything they've got at him. But it's not working: their tails, bogies and leg-weather are having no effect. With one swing of his mighty head, Rick knocks down Large Benjamin, the clock tower! Then he's off again, rampaging wildly through the streets, leaving rubble and destruction in his wake.

I grit my teeth. Gotta stay positive. Gotta get more Toons to safety.

Then it hits me: I can *only see* Rick Ing-Ball.

Where's Bill Dozer?

'FINN MORRIS!' a terrible voice booms behind me. **'SO…**

CHAPTER TWENTY-THREE

END OF THE LINE

The glistening, metal machine-body of President Dozer is bearing down on me.

'I've been looking everywhere for you, my threedy-measurable friend!' he hollers.

I move backwards, but slam straight into a half-destroyed wall.

I'm trapped. There's no way out.

'So, you escaped again, did you?' Dozer cries. **'I was**

planning to deal with you once I'd decimated Toon World, but it looks like I'll have to finish you right now before you can wriggle away again!'

My legs are wobbling so much I can barely stand.

Be brave, Finn, I tell myself. In situations like this, I always used to think: *What would Arley and Tapper do?* But for some reason, the thought that pops into my head right now is: *What would Isha do?*

Isha. My brilliant, brave best friend. Oh, **MONKEY NUTS,** *I hope she's OK.*

Dozer rumbles towards me on his huge clanking tank tracks, his gargant-u-rific BLADE mouth glinting in the sun.

'End of the line, Finn Morris,' he sneers. **'For you and for Toon World.'**

'Why are you doing this?' I shout up at him. 'Why can't you just leave us all alone?'

A look of white-hot FURY spreads across his face. **'BECAUSE YOU RUINED MY CAREER!'**

'What?!' I yell back. 'That doesn't make any sense!'

But Dozer isn't listening any more. His eyes cloud over and he opens his HUMUNGOFIED metal mouth.

I close my eyes. This is it.

End of the line.

CHAPTER TWENTY-FOUR

OR MAYBE NOT

'**T**OOT!!! TOOT!!!!'

Before Bill Dozer can slice and dice me, there's a noise so loud and high-pitched it almost blows my ears off.

A train is thundering at FULL SPEED towards us. A train I recognize . . .

The Runaway Train.

'**What the–**' Dozer tries to move out of its way, but

he's not quick enough. The train PLOUGHS right into him! It crashes into his metal body, sending him flying.

'FINN! OVER HERE!'

A head pops out of the Runaway Train's window. ISHA'S HEAD!

My heart nearly BURSTS out of my chest. 'ISHA!' Happiness explodes inside me like a

TRILLION fireworks. *She's OK!*

She leaps out of the train, and shouts, 'Nice one, RT!'

The Runaway Train chuckles and winks at her. **'No bother, IK!'**

'What . . . ? How . . . ?' There are so many questions pinging around my head. But I don't have time to ask them. Dozer's body sputters and whirrs among the rubble, and with an almighty CREEAKKKKKKKK he's moving again.

Fast. Towards *me*.

'YOU'RE FINISHED, FINN MORRIS!!!'

I look up to see his giant metal mouth opening again. But Isha grabs my hand and pulls me clear. I hear his sharp teeth THUNK into the ground a millimetre from my head!

'COME ON!' Isha yells.

'GET BACK HERE!!' Dozer shouts.

'Get in, you two!' the Runaway Train bellows.

Isha pulls me towards the open train door.

'But that's the RUNAWAY TR—' I start.

'JUST GET IN!' she cries.

I close my eyes and let her drag me on board.

CHAPTER TWENTY-FIVE

THE BIGGEST
BEAR HUG EVER

'Where have you been?! Are you OK?! What happened?!'

Isha just swats all my questions away angrily. 'No time for that now! We need to get to safety!'

'What's the plan, IK?' I hear the Runaway Train yell, as he dodges a massive hole that's been smashed into the pavement – I'm guessing by Rick Ing-Ball's dreadful swinging head.

Isha looks at me. 'Finn?'

'The sewers!' I shout. 'We need to head for the sewers!'

'**Can do!**' the Runaway Train hoots. He screeches around a corner, sending Isha and me flying halfway down the carriage.

'RT!' Isha yells. 'We've talked about this! Control yourself!'

'**Sorry, IK, sorry! Got a bit overexcited. Won't happen again.**'

Isha helps me up from the carriage floor.

'Seriously,' I say, dusting myself off, 'what the **MONKEY NUTS** is happening? Why are you MATES with the Runaway Train?'

'It's like this—' she begins. But at that moment, we zip around another corner to see Jonathan/Ronathan standing over the manhole, guiding terrified Toons down into the sewers.

'RT! Stop!'

The train screeches to a halt and lets us out. Isha pats his window gently. 'Thanks, RT. You're a dude. Finn and me will get as many Toons down to the sewers as we can. You do a full circuit of Toon World – pick up any stragglers and get them straight back here. OK?'

'You got it, IK.' The Runaway Train winks at her and zooms off.

Me and Isha head straight for the manhole, but suddenly – KKERRRRASHHHHHH!!!!! – Rick Ing-Ball's swinging bonce comes smashing through the building in front of us!

We roll out of the way, and I see Jonathan/Ronathan grab the last few Toons and leap down the manhole, closing the cover behind them.

'Quick, in here!' Isha hisses.

Before Rick Ing-Ball can spot us, she pulls me through the half-smashed door of a half-destroyed shoe shop. About fifty scared-looking Toon shoes of all shapes, sizes and colours are hopping out of the back door as we enter, scared senseless by the ghastly skyscraper-sized wrecking machine outside. Me and Isha duck behind the counter, and thankfully, Rick Ing-Ball glides straight past without seeing us.

Isha sighs a mahoosive sigh of relief, and flops down on to the ground. 'Sheesh-a-rooney. That was close.'

I can't stop myself. I fling my arms around her and give her the BIGGEST BEAR HUG ever. 'Isha – I am SO happy to see you that I could literally puke!'

I feel her laugh into my shoulder. 'Please don't.'

I let go of her. 'So, what happened? Where have you been?!'

She shakes bits of crumbled Toon building out of her hair. 'I've been on that train! And it wasn't just *any* train. It was a—'

'Runaway Train! I know!' I say. 'I was so worried! Everyone's been saying that the Runaway Train is a dangerous ruffian!'

She puffs her cheeks out. 'Well, he definitely *was* – at first. We were whizzing about all over Toon World! It was TERRIFYING – he kept zooming right up to the edges of cliffs, and across tiny rickety bridges. I was screaming at him, trying to get him to slow down, but he refused. He said that being fast and wild and out of control was his whole "thing". And I asked: "Why d'you think that is?" And he said it was because his Artist drew him that way, and I told him he didn't always have to do what his Artist told him. I said: "Just because your Artist is wild and reckless and out of control, doesn't mean you have to be!" And he was quite pleased about that – he said that, actually, he wouldn't mind being a bit more calm and chilled out from time to time. Then he asked how come I knew so much about Artists anyway, and I said I was from the Real World . . .' She pauses to take a breath. 'And that *finally* got his attention! He promised me that as long as he could have ten selfies with me he'd take me wherever I wanted to go.'

I can't help giggling with relief. 'They really love their selfies here, don't they?'

'Totes,' she says. 'We became mates after that. I taught him some relaxing breathing techniques that my sister had showed me from her yoga classes. In return, he said he'd take me back to you, but the problem was – I had no idea where you were. But then I saw a rainbow in the sky . . .' She points through the half-crumbling roof above us. 'THAT rainbow.'

'Jenny shot that out of her legs!'

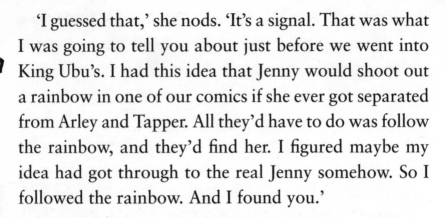

'I guessed that,' she nods. 'It's a signal. That was what I was going to tell you about just before we went into King Ubu's. I had this idea that Jenny would shoot out a rainbow in one of our comics if she ever got separated from Arley and Tapper. All they'd have to do was follow the rainbow, and they'd find her. I figured maybe my idea had got through to the real Jenny somehow. So I followed the rainbow. And I found you.'

I shake my head – half in disbelief at Jenny's brilliant plan, half in guilty sadness. Because hearing Isha say 'one of our comics' has brought back everything that happened before she got on that train. Everything I said to her.

'I'm sorry for getting on that train, Finn,' she murmurs. 'That was stupid.'

'Are you kidding me?!' I shoot back. '*I'm* the one who should be saying sorry! I'm the stupid one! Isha – the stuff I told you about being glad that you were going to America, about how I'm happier drawing comics on my own . . . it was all total BALONEY! The happiest I've ever been in my whole LIFE is when I'm drawing comics with you! You are the greatest friend a numpty like me could ever ask for, and I'm MISERIFIED that you're leaving. That's why I acted like that, and why I said those things. Because I don't want you to go. I'm sorry.'

She smiles. The kind of smile where not just her eyes and mouth are smiling – but her whole FACE is smiling.

'I don't want to go either, Finn,' she says, wiping away a tear that's running down her cheek. 'I want to stay with you. I don't want Finntasmo-Ishazar Comics to end.'

'It won't!' I say, as I remember what Jenny said to me earlier: *You and Isha are MEANT to make comics together.* 'We've got FaceTime, we've got Zoom, we've got email. We can make comics over the internet, easily!'

She grins and nods. 'And I was thinking – this summer, maybe you could come out and visit? We could draw comics together, and then go on a burger-and-milkshake tour of LA!'

I feel my body fill with excitement at the idea. Imagine it: me and Isha in America! 'That would be AWESOME PAWESOME!'

She laughs. 'So, you promise, then? You promise we'll

still be a team? No matter what?'

'Isha,' I say, grabbing her hand. 'Nothing can ever break us apart again.'

And I *really* mean it.

For a second, we just sit there staring at each other, grinning STOOPID grins. And then a HUUUUUUGE crash from outside reminds me that Toon World is still being DESTRUCTIFIED outside.

Our smiles drop. Even though I've finally got my best friend back, it looks like we're both done for . . .

CHAPTER TWENTY-SIX

A GENUINE COMIC BOOK TEAM

'How are we gonna stop them?' Isha asks, once I've filled her in on Bill Dozer and Rick Ing-Ball's evil plan.

'I don't know if we can,' I admit. 'Arley, Tapper and Jenny were giving it their best shot, but even their special moves didn't seem to work against those numpties. They're out there right now, fighting them.' Suddenly a new sense of panic grips me. 'Or at least they were . . .'

What if something's happened to them? I can't think about that now . . .

We both slump down on to the ground, and Isha grabs her leg. 'Ow!' She winces as she pulls out the Magic Pen from her trouser pocket. I'd totally forgotten about it.

'That stupid pen got us into this whole mess,' I grumble.

'Yeah.' Isha's eyes light up suddenly. 'And maybe it can get us out of it . . .'

'How d'you mean?'

She jumps and starts pacing around the room: always a sure-fire sign that Isha Kapesa has a brilliant idea brewing in her brainbox . . .

'We tried to draw the other Toons with it back at the comic shop, right – and it didn't work?'

'You can say that again,' I scoff.

'But remember what Kate Magenta Great Inventor said: **"All we need is a genuine Real World comic book team to draw us with it, and we'll all be zapped back home"**.' She stares at me triumphantly. 'That's it!'

'What's it?' I say.

'We definitely weren't working like a genuine comic book TEAM when we tried it earlier, were we?'

'No, I guess not . . .'

'But we're a team again now, right?'

I jump up. 'You bet your family-sized bag of **MONKEY NUTS** we are!'

'So . . . let's try it again.' She picks up the pen and hands it to me. Then she tears off a big strip of wallpaper from the crumbling shoe shop wall.

'We'd better check this wallpaper isn't ALIVE first,' I say, as a joke.

But quick as a flash, a FACE forms on the wallpaper. **'I very much AM alive, thank you,'** the wallpaper snaps. **'But I don't mind one jot if you doodle on me. In fact, I'll probably rather enjoy it.'**

Isha laughs in disbelief. 'This place is truly BANANAS.'

'OK,' I say. 'Let's draw the Lost Toons.'

Very carefully, I start drawing every member of the Lost Toons, with Isha sitting beside me, describing each one of them perfectly, pointing out little details and characteristics I've forgotten or missed. This time, the pen doesn't fizz or splutter or send out little fireworks. It just . . . draws.

I finish the sketch with all six Lost Toons in it – Zack Jellicoe, Tyger Stylez, GranZilla, Ladder Man, Berry Vinefeld and Kate Magenta Great Inventor. But nothing happens. They don't magically appear.

'I don't think it worked,' I say sadly.

'Rotten luck, chaps,' says the piece of wallpaper. **'Still, I appreciate the nice tattoo you've given me.'**

'Hang on a sec.' Isha takes the pen off me. 'Let's give it one final touch . . .'

Over the top of my drawing, she writes: *A Finntasmo-Ishazar Comic.*

From outside comes a super LOUD crash.

And then the door of our building is BOOTED off its hinges.

'You took your time!' Zack Jellicoe booms, the Lost Toons grinning behind him.

CHAPTER TWENTY-SEVEN

THE BATTLE OF TOON WORLD

'It worked! I can't believe it WORKED!'

Me and Isha are running behind the Lost Toons in the direction of Bill Dozer and Rick Ing-Ball. As soon as the six of them magically appeared, we told them about the baddies trying to destroy Toon World and they SPRANG straight into action.

'I'm guessing that's them?' says Kate Magenta, pointing her paw at the giant machines tearing up trees and houses two streets away.

'You guessed right,' Isha shouts.

'Well, they won't last long against the might of the Lost Toons!' Zack yells, zipping left and right on his skateboard ahead of us.

'Straight up!' bellows Ladder Man.

'Very true, dear,' says GranZilla.

'What's red and juicy and goes up and down? A strawberry in a lift!' chuckles Berry Vinefeld.

'Berry - seriously, mate - now is NOT the time,' Tyger Stylez snaps.

We all screech round the corner and suddenly Dozer and Ing-Ball are RIGHT there, crushing and stomping

and destructifying everything in sight.

'Hey – who are those three brave Toons trying to stop them?' Zack asks.

'ARLEY! TAPPER!' I cry.

'JENNY WEATHERLEGS!' Isha shouts.

Our three characters turn as they hear our voices. They're all ragged and covered in dust and bits of rubble. They look like they've been having the fight of their LIVES.

But they're OK!

'We've brought back-up!' I yell at them.

'Too right they have!' shouts Zack. 'Lost Toons . . . ATTACK!'

He TEARS past me on his skateboard, launches off an overturned car and KICKFLIPS right into Bill Dozer's horrible face!

Tyger Stylez follows him – bouncing up into a tall tree and

then aiming an AWESOME kung-fu kick straight at Rick Ing-Ball's head! GranZilla puts her knitting down carefully, and breathes FIRE!

Ladder Man leans his ginormous ladder against the side of a skyscraper, scurries up it, and starts trying to

rip out cogs and other bits of machinery from Dozer's control panel on the back of his head.

All of this while Tapper's bogies are FLYING, Arley's

tail is WHIZZING and Jenny is shooting HAILSTONES, THUNDER and LIGHTNING out of her legs!

'I TOLD you that pen worked, didn't I?' Kate Magenta Great Inventor nudges her llama head between us and gives us a cheeky wink.

'Yeah – we just needed the secret ingredient,' Isha says. 'Teamwork!'

'Exactly. Now, if you'll excuse me, I really should be pulling my weight in this battle too.' She reaches into her white lab coat and pulls out three sticks of dynamite and a beaker full of bubbly green liquid, labelled 'VERY EXPLOSIVE'. **'In a jiffy . . .'**

'Should we be doing something too?' Isha asks, as we watch Kate launching her explosives at Rick Ing-Ball's gargant-u-rific body. Only Berry Vinefeld is still stood next to us, a big grin on his raspberry face. He doesn't really seem to get the seriousness of the situation . . .

'What could we do?' I say to Isha. 'We don't have any superpowers. Anyway, I'm sure these guys can handle it . . .'

But the truth is . . . I'm not sure of that at all. Rick Ing-Ball swats Jenny out of the air, sending her crashing into a nearby hedge. Bill Dozer flicks Ladder Man off his neck and nearly chops GranZilla in half with his blade. Tyger Stylez and Zack are already flat on their backs, after being WHACKED by Rick's swinging bonce.

The truth is . . . *we're losing.*

The good guys are losing.

Isha grabs my hand. She must sense this is the end too. Well, if it really IS the end, I'm not just standing here and watching.

'Isha, come on,' I say. 'Let's go and join them.'

But at that moment I realize someone else is way ahead of us.

CHAPTER TWENTY-EIGHT

WHAT A GREAT AUDIENCE

'Berry, wait!' Isha shouts. 'It's too dangerous!'

But Berry Vinefeld is not listening. He waddles towards the mayhem until he reaches the base of Rick Ing-Ball's gigantic wheels. He looks SO tiny next to the towering villains. He's so small that I don't think the bad guys have even noticed him. He pulls out his little microphone, taps it to make sure it's working. And then he speaks.

'Hey, good evening, ladies and robo-baddies, what a great audience,' he chuckles.

Dozer and Ing-Ball stop their ghastly demolishing and stare down at him. 'You know,' Berry says, 'I went to the shops yesterday to try and buy some blueberries, but they were all out. You might say it was a . . . fruitless trip!'

For a second or two, there is complete silence. It's like the two baddies can't even believe what they've just heard. But then both of them start shaking and whirring, like their insides are stuffed with jellied eels.

'That's . . . that's the worst joke I've ever heard . . .' Rick Ing-Ball stutters.

Bill Dozer begins juddering and fizzling. 'Oh God! It's so painfully unfunny! The pain! The pain! I can't take it . . .'

'A fruitless trip, a fruitless trip,' Ing-Ball keeps repeating, as bits of machinery start to tumble out of his metal belly...

Both the bad guys spark and sputter and shake until …

They change back!

They shrrrrrrink back down to their ordinary size and lie there, dazed, on the pavement!

Me, Isha and all the Toons are staring at Berry Vinefeld in INCREDU-TASTIC AMAZEMENT.

'Berry . . .' Kate says. **'You DID it!'**

And then all of us rush to give the fruity little hero a hug.

CHAPTER TWENTY-NINE

WHY?

We all bear hug Berry so hard we risk turning him into a SMOOTHIE.

And then a bright beam of yellow light catches my eye. I look round to see Jenny Weatherlegs shooting SUNSHINE out of her toes as she grins the WIDEST grin you've ever seen at Isha. **'Isha . . . it's really you!'**

Isha looks totally overwhelmed. Like she's so full of HAPPINESS that it might start to spill out of her at any moment. It makes *me* happy just to see it. I remember how ridonkulously incredible it was when I first met Arley and Tapper.

The two of them hug.

'That rainbow idea . . .' Isha grins. 'Inspired!'

'It was all you, Ishe,' Jenny shoots back.

'Hey, let's leave the mushy stuff till later,' says Tyger Stylez. **'Those two baddies are waking up . . .'**

In the middle of the rubble-strewn street, Bill Dozer and Rick Ing-Ball are groaning and moaning in a villainous heap.

Zack, Tyger and Arley are over them, quick as a flash. **'Don't even THINK about moving, you nefarious numpties,'** Arley hisses.

'Tell us why you did this!' Zack shouts. **'What made you want to destroy Toon World?'**

Dozer blinks up at us. The smarmy evil smirk is gone now. His face just looks blank, and his head is twitching like a robot that's had a bottle of Fanta poured into its circuits.

'DESTROY TOON WORLD, DESTROY TOON WORLD,' he drones in a monotonous robotic voice. 'DESTROY FINN MORRIS, DESTROY FINN MORRIS . . .'

'What?!' I gawp at him. 'Why?!'

'You are a bit of a doofus, to be fair, Finnbot,' Tapper says.

'It must be their Artist!' Jenny cries.

'She's right,' Isha nods. 'Jenny got the rainbow idea because she shares that connection with me. The Runaway Train is wild because his Artist draws him like that . . . So these two must have the same connection with *their* Artist – he or she is feeding them this desire to destroy Toon World and Finn!'

Zack turns back to the baddies. 'Who's your Artist?'

But suddenly I know the answer. I understand why Bill Dozer seemed to know me – to know that I'm a cartoonist. I think back to what he told me earlier: 'YOU DESTROYED MY ENTIRE CAREER!'

The hairs on the back of my neck are tingling. I look at Isha, and she's staring back at me like she's realized it, too. We both shout it at the exact same time:

'YORKY!'

'*He* planned to destroy Toon World!' Isha gasps. 'Even if it meant destroying his own characters in the process.'

Arley smirks at me. **'I TOLD you he was still plotting his dastardly revenge!'**

My brain is whizzing fourteen jillion miles per second. Yorky is still out there, somewhere! And he wants revenge on me for ruining his career. He's so bitter and twisted that he created these characters – Bill Dozer and Rick Ing-Ball – and filled them with his resentment for comics and cartoons, his hatred for everything in Toon World. And for me.

We might have beaten him this time, but I know for sure he won't stop. Me and Isha have to try and find him. To defeat him once and for all.

If we can ever get back to the Real World, that is . . .

'Hey – what's that noise?' Kate says suddenly. The air is full of murmuring voices, and the trump-trump-trump of a thousand footsteps.

We all turn towards where the sound is coming from to see Jonathan/Ronathan striding towards us, a mahoosive crowd of smiling Toons following them.

CHAPTER THIRTY

YOU DON'T SMELL GREAT

I'm so CHUFFED to see them safe and sound I actually run up and give Jonathan/Ronathan a big hug.

'You guys did it! You got everyone to safety!' And then I flinch. 'Wow. You, erm, don't smell great . . .'

'We HAVE just been down in the sewers,' grins Jonathan.

'Yeah, cut us some slack,' grins Ronathan. They both

look EXACTLY identical now that Ronathan's smiling.

From the back of the crowd, we hear an ear-splittingly loud **'TOOT! TOOT!'** The Runaway Train pulls up in a cloud of steam, his doors hissing open to let out more safe-and-sound Toon Worlders!

'RT!' Isha thumps the train's door triumphantly. 'You did it!'

'I'm sorry, I'm confused,' says Jonathan. **'I was under the impression the Runaway Train was a dangerous ruffian?'**

'I used to be,' says RT. **'Until a good friend named Isha Kapesa taught me to think for myself. I will not let my Artist's reckless behaviour control me any longer! From this day forward, I'm not the RUNAWAY TRAIN – I'm the RELIABLE TRAIN!'**

'Oh, RT, you're the greatest!' Isha cries.

Around us, the streets are

packed with Toons again – not panicking or screaming this time, but laughing and hugging and jumping for joy that they survived. The Lost Toons are at the centre of it all, being swamped by Toon friends they haven't seen for YEARS. I feel a warm glow in my chest as I watch them.

We did it. We got them home.

A few members of the Toon Police Department move through the crowd, following Zack Jellicoe, and handcuff Bill Dozer and Rick Ing-Ball – who are both still spluttering, '**DESTROY TOON WORLD**' over and over again.

Beside me, I feel Isha's arm round my shoulder. 'Well, we defeated the bad guys, saved countless Toon Worlders and got the Lost Toons home again. Not too shabby for a day's work, I'd say?'

I nod. 'Yeah. But we've still got no clue how you and me can get back to the Real World. And also – we may have saved the Toon Worlders, but look at Toon World itself . . .'

We both stare around the destructified landscape. It's all half-collapsed buildings, toppled trees and ripped-up roads.

Isha purses her lips thoughtfully. 'Yeah. I've been thinking about that. D'you remember that map we found, just after we arrived here?'

'Yeah. The map of Toon World?'

She raises her eyebrows and grins at me. 'Well, if the Magic Pen brought back the Lost Toons, I don't see why it can't bring back Toon World too.'

CHAPTER THIRTY-ONE

A NEW MAP

A few minutes later, Isha and me are sat in front of another much bigger sheet of talking Toon wallpaper, about to start our BIGGEST CARTOON PROJECT YET. I've got Kate's Magic Pen gripped tightly in my hand. Around us, a MAHOOSIVE crowd of Toon Worlders are watching in anticipation.

'OK,' I say. 'So . . . where do I start?'

Jonathan points to the centre of the paper. **'How about starting with Large Benjamin, the clock tower? He's one of the most famous sites of Toon World.'**

'Technically, Large Benjamin is actually the name of the bell inside the clock tower,' says Ronathan smugly.

'That's right, brother!' Jonathan beams. **'Superb Toon Tourism knowledge!'**

'Thanks, brother!'

I remember the giraffe train guard pointing the clock tower out to me just after Isha got on that train. I start

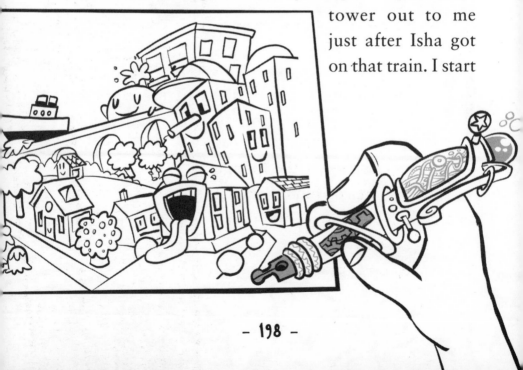

sketching it, with Jonathan, Ronathan and the other Toons all describing little details I might have missed.

And when I've finished – I don't want to blow my own trumpet – but it looks pretty flippin' *awesome*.

'**Look!**' Ronathan shouts. We all follow his gaze. On the horizon, the half-crumbled clock tower has magically reappeared – good as new!

'**Hello there!**' booms the clock face.

'It's working!' Isha cries. 'Everyone – tell Finn what to draw next!'

One by one, bit by bit, the Toons describe each area of Toon World – each building and street and park – and I carefully redraw the map. And one by one, bit by bit, the real

Toon World rebuilds itself before our eyes! The LOL-O-SSEUM springs back to life, chuckling away on the horizon, as I sketch it. The Trifle Tower bursts back on to the landscape, its cream and jelly looking even more

bouncy and colourful than before! I draw CelebriToon Village from Tapper's description and it pops back up on a hill in the distance.

All around us, houses and towers and bridges are leaping up out of nowhere as I doodle them! It's utterly butterly INCREDIBLE – seeing the things I'm sketching literally coming to life as I work!

'Can you draw us a cheeky Starbucks as well, Finnbot?' Tapper asks. **'I looooove me an ice-cold Frappuccino after a hard day's battling bad guys.'**

'All right, but just a small one.'

'I've really outdone myself with that pen,' Kate Magenta says, as I put the finishing touches to Tapper's Starbucks. **'It's deffo my greatest invention ever.'** She winks at me. **'Although your drawing skills aren't bad either, Finn.'**

'Cheers!'

With the map now fully redrawn, I hand the Magic Pen back to her. But she shakes her shaggy llama head. **'No, no. You guys hang on to it. You might need it again sometime. After all, it was designed to be used by a** genuine comic book team . . .'

Me and Isha look at each other, both our smiles so big that they're in danger of stretching into our ears.

'So, all's well that ends well, eh?' chuckles Tapper.

'Well, yeah,' says Tyger Stylez. 'Although Finn and Isha are still stuck in Toon World with no hope of ever getting home.'

Tapper blows a raspberry at him. 'That's no biggie. They can sleep on our sofa!'

Isha looks at me. 'I did have one idea for that, actually. It's a long shot, but . . .'

She leans in and whispers in my ear. I burst out laughing when I hear her suggestion.

It's so BANANAS that it might just work . . .

On the map, in the centre of Clowning Street, I sketch exactly what she's just described to me . . .

I hear a gasp of amazement and look up from the map.

It's there. Shimmering and glowing on the pavement next to us.

The Real World Portal.

CHAPTER THIRTY-TWO

THROUGH THE PORTAL

'**T**his means you have to come back and visit!' Tapper shouts. '**Every weekend!**'

Isha cracks up laughing. 'I'm not sure about EVERY weekend, Taps. But we'll be back.' She grins at Jenny. 'You can bet your boots we'll be back . . .'

'**I can't thank you both enough for getting us home,**' Zack says, giving us both a hug. '**We owe you big time.**'

'**Totes,**' says Tyger Stylez, as he and Ladder Man high-five us. **'You guys are awesome.'**

'In a jiffy!' chirps Kate Magenta. **'And give us a shout if you ever need a hand taking down this Yorky fellow.'**

'Ooh yes, he sounds AWFUL, dear,' says GranZilla.

'We will,' I say. 'And I was thinking – since you guys have all lost your Artists . . . how would you feel about Isha and me drawing you in our comics?'

The Lost Toons make it clear how they'd feel by giving us a ROAR of approval!

'Even me?' squeaks Berry Vinefeld.

'Of course, Berry!' Isha rubs his cheeky little raspberry head. 'You're the hero of the day, after all.'

Berry dances a jig on the spot. **'Oh, THANK YOU, ladies and gentlemen, you've been a WONDERFUL audience! And hey, you'll like this one - what did the blackberry say when he was off on a long walk? "I'm going for a bramble!"'**

I try very hard not to groan. 'That's great stuff, Berry.'

'I'll try to come up with some less cringeworthy fruit-based gags when we start drawing him,' Isha whispers.

Then Jenny, Arley and Tapper are in front of us, giving us the TIGHTEST hugs ever, and we know it's really time to go.

'Bye, Jenny!'

'Bye, Isha!'

'Laters, IK!'

'See you, RT!'

'Ta-ra, Finnbot! Come back any time for a Frappuccino!'

'Cheery-bye, Finn Morris,' Arley winks, giving me a fist bump. 'Until our next adventure together . . .'

We wave them all one final goodbye, before we take a deep breath and step through the portal.

CHAPTER THIRTY-THREE

BACK

The feeling is like being fed through a blender, squeezed through a cheese grater, then BLASTED at full power in a microwave. All at the same time.

But it only lasts a couple of seconds.

And then . . . darkness.

A cold, hard floor.

I open my eyes and look around me. Empty magazine racks, tatty posters on the ivy-covered walls. A weird, damp smell . . .

'We're back, Finn!' Isha shouts. 'We're back in King Ubu's Comic Book Store!'

The shop looks exactly the same as it did when we left, with one pretty MAJOR exception. Burnt into the wall is now a shining, shimmering magical doorway, with the words 'TOON WORLD PORTAL' glowing above it.

'We really can go back to Toon World,' Isha whispers.

'We should probably, y'know . . . cover this up,' I suggest. 'In case anyone else finds it.'

We stack a load of boxes in front of the portal so it's fully hidden. As we walk out of the shop, I take one look back, wondering when I'll next be stepping through it . . .

Outside, the sun is still shining brightly. It feels beyond weird to

see the real, threedy-
measurable world again, having
spent so long in a 2D cartoon landscape.

'Finn! Isha! Over here!'

It's Mona. She's sat in her car, exactly where she let us out. But that must have been HOURS ago.

'So sorry, sis,' Isha says, as we scramble into the back seat. 'You must have been waiting ages . . .'

Mona wrinkles her forehead. 'What are you on about, Ishe? You've only been in there five minutes.'

We gawp at each other. And then I remember something the giraffe train guard told me at the station: *The whole concept of 'time' doesn't really exist here in Toon World . . .*

'Did you have fun?' Mona asks, as she starts the engine.

'Erm . . .' Isha looks up at the sky. The rainbow is still there, sparkling above us. 'Yeah, that's one word for it . . .'

Back at Isha's, we flop on to her bed in TOTAL exhaustion.

'Well,' she says. 'I don't know about you, but that was definitely the longest five minutes of *my* life.'

I laugh. 'Yep. What an adventure. And it's wild about Bill Dozer and Rick Ing-Ball. They were Yorky's puppets this whole time.'

She sits up. 'Yorky won't stop, Finn. We may have won this battle, but he still wants a full-scale war. He's still out to destroy Toon World – and get his revenge on you.' She takes a deep breath: 'We're going to have to find out where he is. Stop him once and for all.'

'Why are you saying "we"?' I ask, with a grin. 'You'll be off swanning about in "Los Angeles", won't you? You'll have forgotten all about me pretty soon . . .'

She folds her arms and pouts at me. 'Don't start that again, Finn Morris. We're a team, aren't we? No matter how far away we are from each other.'

'Course we are. I just . . .' I feel myself going red as I stare into the duvet. Half of me feels embarrassed and wants to stop talking. But, no. I have to say this.

'I'm really gonna miss you, that's all.'

I feel her throw her arms around me. 'I'm really gonna miss you too, Finn,' she whispers.

And as I hug her back, I feel THIRTY FEET TALL. She's my best pal. And she always will be.

She breaks away and smiles at me. 'But I'm not leaving for another three weeks, which means we've still got plenty of time to make more comics.'

'Well, what are we waiting for, then? Let's crack on with the next Finntasmo-Ishazar production!'

We pull up our chairs at her desk and I turn to a fresh sheet in my sketchbook. That familiar old tingly electricity surges through me. This – right here – this is the best feeling in the world.

'So . . .' I ask her. 'How does it start?

CHAPTER THIRTY-FOUR

EPILOGUE

Three months later, on a dark and cloudy Wednesday afternoon, I'm sat in my bedroom putting the finishing touches to the latest Finntasmo-Ishazar comic.

Isha left for America two months ago now, but we've still managed to produce at least one comic a week ever since! We have MAHOOSIVE five-or-six-hour ideas brainstorms over FaceTime where we write the scripts together, and think of stories and characters and jokes, and then I'll go off and draw them up.

Tonight I'm doing the final panels for our newest adventure. I'm due to FaceTime Isha in a minute so I can show it to her. It's still early in the morning for her over in Los Angeles, but we're gonna get in a quick chat now before she heads to her new school. I can't wait to see her.

The truth is: I miss her.

A lot.

OK, OK . . . A RIDONKULOUS LOT.

But in a weird way, it feels like she still lives just down the road. We're just as close as ever, we see each other every day, and I don't want to blow my own trumpet here, but I actually think our comics have got even better! Everyone at my school is still loving Arley and Tapper's adventures, and now, thanks to Isha, we've also got an international audience. She's been handing our comics out at her new school in Los Angeles, and people are loving them there too!

It's funny, I thought I'd feel sad and lonely listening to her talk about her new life in the USA, but actually it's exciting.

I'm excited for her.

I still haven't been back to King Ubu's Comic Book Store, though. Now that the Lost Toons are back in Toon World, the shop is completely empty, with the secret glimmering, shimmering portal still hidden inside it. Any time I want, I could step through it and I'd be right back in Toon World, with all my wild and wacky two-dimensional chums. But it feels wrong to go back without Isha.

She's coming back to England soon to visit family, so maybe we'll pay Arley, Tapper and Jenny a visit then . . . The idea fills me with bubbly excitement as I keep scribbling away in my sketchbook.

The one thing we HAVEN'T talked about in ages is Yorky. Before Isha left, we made a vow to try and track him down before he tried to destroy Toon World again. But we've not really got any further with it. Sometimes, in the middle of the night, I'll still feel hot with worry that he's out there, somewhere, plotting and planning . . .

As I sketch the very last line of our new comic, my

laptop lights up.

BEE-BEEP-BOOP-BOOP! It's Isha calling on FaceTime!

Tingling with joy at the thought of seeing my best pal, I click 'ANSWER'. Her grinning face appears on screen.

'FINN!'

'ISHA! So great to see you! How's LA?'

She swats the question back at me through the screen. 'No time for small talk! You'll never guess what's happened. I've got the most AMAZING news!'

'Oh yeah?' I ask. 'What is it?'

'You know I've been giving out our comics to the kids at my new school?'

'Yeah.'

'Well, one of their parents is a top film producer – and he saw our latest comic, and he LOVES it!'

I lean back on my chair, trying to take this news in. 'Wow. Seriously?'

'Yes!' Isha cries. 'And guess what . . . He wants to

make an ARLEY & TAPPER MOVIE!' She leans her face so close to the screen I can see every tooth in her smile. 'Finn – you need to get on the next plane to HOLLYWOOD!'

ACKNOWLEDGEMENTS

A MAHOOSIVE thank you firstly to Phil Corbett for his truly phenomenal illustrations, and bringing all the new characters to life so fantastically. And to Steve Wells for his stunning design wizardry, too.

Mega-sized thanks, as well, to the editorial legend that is Rachel Leyshon, for her endless stream of brilliant ideas and being such a joy to work with. To everyone at Chicken House, too: a writer couldn't wish for a nicer publisher! Thanks so much to Barry, Elinor, Rachel H, Esther, Jazz, Kesia, Laura, Sarah and Olivia.

For their kind words, encouragement and work on the first book, I'd also like to say a big thanks to Marzena Currie and Petroula Gavriilidou.

Thanks to my awesome agent Clare Wallace for everything, and to Lucy Ivison for being a top-drawer idea-bouncer-offer and all-round good egg.

And much love to Carolina and Maudushka.

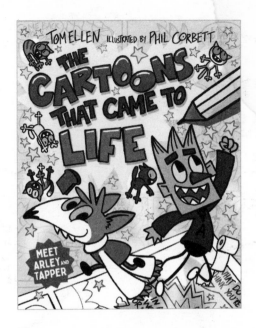

THE CARTOONS THAT CAME TO LIFE
Illustrated by Phil Corbett

Finn Morris dreams of being a famous cartoonist. Or at least he used to. When bullies rip up his sketchbook, Finn quits – he even stops drawing his favourite characters, Arley and Tapper.

So, imagine how he feels the next day when he wakes up to see Arley and Tapper staring straight back at him! Cartoons don't just appear in the real world . . . do they? But if they did, what would happen? And how on earth would you send them back?!

'. . . a warm-hearted story about friendship, facing down your worries and being true to who you are.'
THE WEEK JUNIOR

Paperback, ISBN 978-1-910002-88-9, £6.99 • ebook, ISBN 978-1-913322-42-7, £6.99

MILTON THE MIGHTY by EMMA READ
Illustrated by ALEX G GRIFFITHS

When spider Milton discovers he's been branded deadly, he fears for his life and his species. Alongside his buddies, big hairy Ralph and daddy-long-legs Audrey, he decides to clear his name. But to succeed, Milton must befriend his house human, Zoe. Is Milton mighty enough to achieve the impossible?

'. . . a charming and thoughtful read.'
THE SCOTSMAN

Paperback, ISBN 978-1-911490-81-4, £6.99 • ebook, ISBN 978-1-912626-31-1, £6.99

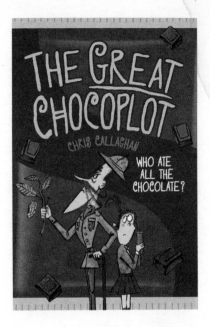

THE GREAT CHOCOPLOT by CHRIS CALLAGHAN

It's the end of chocolate – for good! A chocolate mystery . . . At least that's what they're saying on TV. Jelly and her gran are gobsmacked – they love a Blocka Choca bar or two. But then a train of clues leads back to a posh chocolate shop in town owned by the distinctly bitter Garibaldi Chocolati. Is it really the chocopocalypse, or a chocoplot to be cracked?

'With an excellent cast of characters, laugh-out-loud moments, and witty and sharp observations, this is a great choice for fans of Dahl and Walliams.'
THE GUARDIAN

Paperback, ISBN 978-1-910002-51-3, £6.99 • ebook, ISBN 978 -1-910655-57-3, £6.99

GRANNY MAGIC by ELKA EVALDS
Illustrated by TEEMU JUHANI

Will's beloved granny made cakes and knitted itchy jumpers – that's what he thought. But when she passes away and dodgy Jasper Fitchet moves in to their village, dark magic begins to unravel in Knittington. Can Will and his gran's old craft group tie Fitchet in knots? With the help of her old motorbike and a flock of magical sheep, they might just do it . . . so long as they don't drop a stitch.

'This joyous celebration of spinning and spells features motorbike stunts and gold-fleeced sheep.'
THE GUARDIAN

Paperback, ISBN 978-1-912626-19-9, £6.99 • ebook, ISBN 978-1-912626-65-6, £6.99

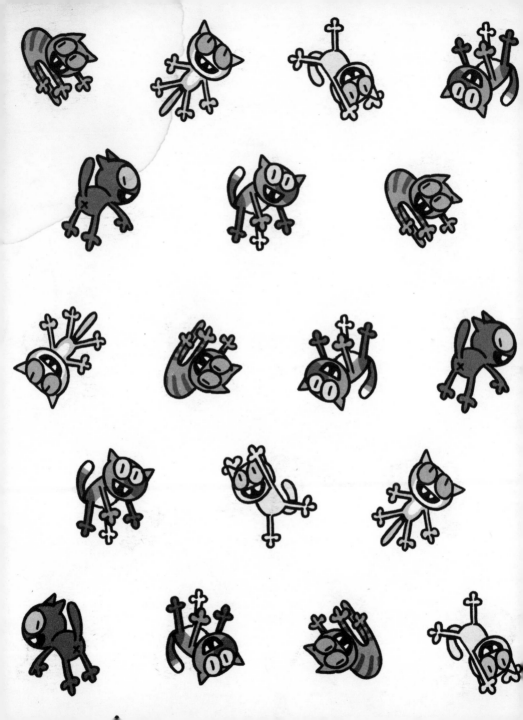

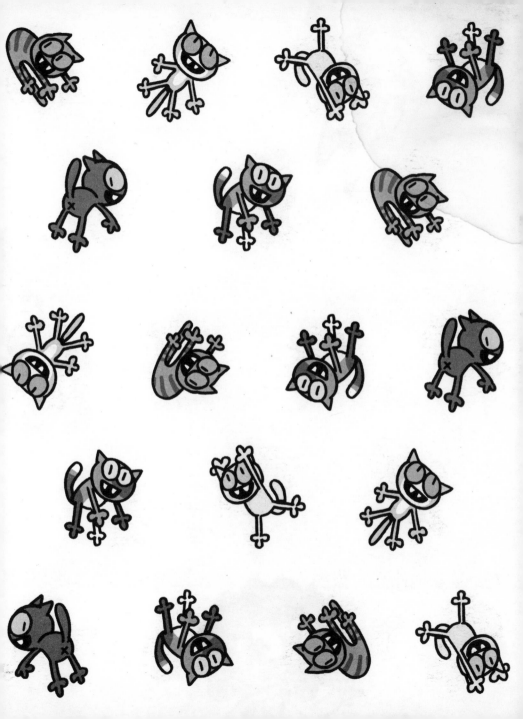